ABOUT THE AUTHOR

KATHLEEN PEYTON started writing at the age of nine and had her first book accepted for publication when she was fifteen. While she was at school in London, she daydreamed of owning her own pony, and so horses became the subject of many of her books.

Kathleen originally studied to become an artist, but she also continued to write and has since had more than fifty books published. She has won both the Carnegie Medal and the Guardian Children's Fiction Prize, and her best known books, the original *Flambards* trilogy, were made into a television series.

She now lives with her husband and her horses near Maldon in Essex.

To find out more about K. M. Peyton, log on to www.kmpeyton.co.uk

FAR FROM HOME

K. M. PEYTON

USBORNE

First published in the UK in 2009 by Usborne Publishing Ltd., Usborne House,
83-85 Saffron Hill, London EC1N 8RT, England. www.usborne.com

The right of K. M. Peyton to be identified as the author of this
work has been asserted by her in accordance with the
Copyright, Designs and Patents Act, 1988.

Cover photography: model supplied by Looks London Ltd./
photo by Steve Shott; background: sky by Digital Vision, hills by Adam Woolfitt
© Robert Harding Picture Library/Alamy.

Artwork by Ian McNee.

The name Usborne and the devices ♀ ⊕ are Trade Marks of
Usborne Publishing Ltd.

A CIP catalogue record for this book is available from the British Library.

First published in America in 2012 AE.

PB ISBN 9780794532925   ALB ISBN 9781601302878

JFMAMJJAS ND/12 01483/1 Printed in Dongguan, Guangdong, China.

I

The cohort commanded by Theodosius Valerian Aquila, some five hundred strong, marched out of Camulodunum on a bright, sharp autumn morning. They were leaving, heading for Hadrian's wall some four hundred miles north and the whole town turned out to cheer them on their way. They made a splendid sight beneath the proud standard. The metalwork of their uniforms glittered in the sunlight, the bronze helmets glowed beneath crimson plumes, their nailed sandals slapped in perfect unison on the hard road. At their head marched Theodosius himself, his black eyes shining with joy, very much aware that the town rulers returning his departing salute were only too pleased to see him go. He had not endeared himself to the powers-that-be during his short term in their city. But his men loved him and the people of the town were full of admiration for his spirit and courage (and not least for his stunning good looks) so their cheers were full of genuine emotion.

And no one in the crowd was more moved than the fifteen-year-old servant girl Minna, who had taken a solemn leave of him the night before. They had been friends from childhood, the governor's son and the servant's daughter, but their ways had separated as the boy had been schooled for high office and command in the army, and the girl had learned only sewing and cooking and how to stay in her place.

But the friendship had been constant. Minna had loved Theo ever since she could remember. She had known this day of his departure was imminent, and had come out early with the crowd to see him go. Her mistress, the tribune's daughter Julia, was in the crowd too somewhere, but in the excitement they had soon lost each other. Minna only had eyes for Theo.

Pushing and shoving her way through the raucous townsfolk, she was unprepared for the panic that started to overwhelm her as she saw, not only Theo, but all the people most dear in her life departing with him: her brother Cerdic and her sometime friend Draco, both soldiers, Theo's slave Benoc and dear Stuf, her soulmate from home. Jostled and crushed in the crowd as she fought to keep up with the passing army, her dismay started to choke her. As the men passed through the great Balkerne Gate on to the road heading north, the townspeople started to drop away, but then Minna saw the army horses go by: her own darling Silva whom she had brought up and trained herself, and Theo's horse, the chestnut stallion Caractacus... it was too terrible, seeing them go! She started to sob, running and stumbling, too tear-blind to see what she was doing. The baggage train rumbled by, the big wagons pulled by oxen carrying all the army gear, the food, the tenting, the slaves and women and all the raggle-taggle that always attached itself to an army on the move. Scarcely knowing what she was doing, Minna made a lunge for one of the last wagons, hauling herself up by the tailboard and clinging on for dear life. She must go too! Even as she hung there the question thumped through her brain: what was she doing? She was out of her mind!

By all the blessings of the gods, the wagon she fell into was not the one full of slaves and servants but the wagon that carried the tenting for the camps at night. Reposing comfortably on the top, hands behind his head, was her old friend Stuf. He sat up, caught her arm and pulled her in, laughing at her precipitous arrival. Nothing ever fazed Stuf.

"Oh, Stuf, what have I done?" Minna was half laughing, half crying.

"Are you sure you're doing the right thing?" he inquired.

"No, I'm not!" Minna squeaked.

"Well, you can always go back if you change your mind."

Stuf was always a giver of sane advice. He was in the baggage train legally, employed as a skilled hunter by the goodwill of the army commander. He thought that the same Theodosius Valerian Aquila would not be thrilled to know that one-time servant girl Minna had elected to follow him after he had taken a solemn farewell of her.

"Do you think he will be furious if he finds out?"

Minna asked him. "I daren't show myself!"

"He's hardly likely to see you here. You've got the whole cohort between the two of you. He's marching in front and you're in the last cart. By the time he finds out you're with us, we'll be halfway to Caledonia."

Stuf's innate good sense was always calming. He had never joined the army like most of the young men, but lived his own life on the Essex shore, beach-combing, supplying fish to the women, hunting in the forest. He had never known his parents. He had the quick senses of an animal, and a surprising gentleness considering the harshness of his life. He had elected to follow the army because Theodosius was his friend and he was bored, at seventeen, and looking for something else in his life. Minna had known him since she was a baby. Finding him in the cart she had chosen to scramble into seemed like a sign from the gods that her decision was the right one. All the same, her brain was whirling. She had accepted her farewell from Theo the night before and had only gone out to wave goodbye! She had been quite unprepared for the emotion that had overwhelmed her: to see Theo march out of her life. It wasn't possible! She had run...

"Oh, Stuf, he will be so angry!"

Stuf laughed. "You are stupid. He will have to act angry, but of course he will be pleased. How could he not be? To have a girl like you chasing him? Everyone knows he loves you. Why else would he have risked his life, fighting Cintus, to save you – and nearly risked his career as well? That was the crux – to risk his career, disobeying orders, when everyone knows his career comes first with him, even before you."

Minna sat digesting Stuf's words: *everyone knows he loves you. Everyone*…yet she scarcely knew that herself. He had never said so, never touched her beyond a brotherly arm around her shoulder…once, under his cloak in the rain, she had felt his heart beating against her own…it made her feel faint now, to remember that. But the way he looked at her, yes…the words he didn't say, the blood he had shed for her, fighting Cintus, the wild barbarian who had held her captive. It seemed so, to other people, that he loved her. But would he ever tell her so? Minna had loved him all her life, ever since they had played together as children in the fort at Othona.

"I can't stand being a lady's maid! Anything is better than that. I had to come."

"Oh, Minna, will you ever be satisfied? You ran

away in the first place because you were being forced to marry Esca – an ugly, ignorant fellow, admitted, but rich enough, with a house to offer you and rich parents. You ran away and were lucky enough to get a job with the tribune's daughter, with – again – a fine house to live in and good food to eat. Now you've done it again."

"I've always run away to be near Theo."

That was the truth. Stuf grinned.

"If I were you, I'd volunteer for the army. They all want to follow him too. Join the ranks. You're as tough as most of them."

Minna laughed. Already, with Stuf's good-humored company, she was feeling that her wild escapade might not be so terrible. Her pounding heart had calmed. She was sitting on a great mattress made up of the leather tenting that would be erected each night for the soldiers' shelter. If she had been unlucky she would have jumped into a wagon full of slaves and servants who wouldn't have made her welcome, or a wagon full of salted cod and pickled onions. As it was, she lolled like a Roman lady on her comfortable bedding, rocked pleasantly by the grumbling progress of the faithful oxen. The sun shone through the canvas roofing, making leafy patterns that jiggled and danced to the wagon's movement, and the distant, rhythmic slap of the cohort's iron-studded sandals on the hard road made a soothing beat. Her panic had died away, although her mind still raced as she considered her future. Theo was looking to fight and had a whole army now to play with: not much hope that she could find a job there. She was just a camp follower, one of the despised bunch of women who trailed after moving armies.

She lay back sleepily on her soft bed. With every step the oxen took she was more and more sure she had done the right thing. Silva and Caractacus were being led by grooms a little way in front of the wagon she was in. Soon she was impatient with lying in her soft bed and decided to get down and walk and see her horses.

"Stuf, get down with me. I want to see what's going on."

Stuf grumbled: "Just walking along a road – that's all that's going on."

But he slithered off the bed as she jumped down and joined her on the road. It was at a point where the route was starting up a long, gradual hill, so that they could see ahead of them the whole cohort marching. It was a stirring sight, the five hundred men in perfect formation, the sun glinting off their helmets, the standard bravely glittering. Two men marched at their head, one of them Theo, the other his second-in-command, Titus.

"You'd think he'd ride," Stuf said. "It's his privilege, after all, as commander."

"He won't take privileges," Minna said. No wonder they loved him, she thought, when they saw him enduring the same hardships as themselves. Their packs, shields and full armor made a heavy burden and they had to march twenty miles a day. They would halt every hour for several minutes, during which time the slower-moving baggage animals caught up.

Minna was glad Stuf was at her side as she noticed the stir that went around the raggle-taggle of women that made up the backmarkers of the train when they saw her. They were mostly the centurions' women and slaves. Legally they were not supposed to be there, but it was almost impossible to apply the law and a blind eye was usually turned; they often made themselves useful, after all. Minna knew several of them by sight, and a few of the slaves and servants she had spoken to. There was an older woman she liked called Occa, the partner of an old soldier called Gaius, and surely Theo's devoted slave Benoc was there – but she couldn't see him.

"Did Benoc come?" she asked Stuf.

She knew Benoc had dreaded leaving Camulodunum and taking to the road. Had he defected at the last moment and run home? But surely he would never leave Theo, whom he loved as dearly as she did? She and Benoc were forever in competition for Theo's regard. Once she had been deeply jealous of Benoc for his closeness to Theo, but over time she had come to admire him for the devotion he showed when Theo treated him as he had a right to treat his slave, with cruel disregard. Who would be a slave? Benoc was a Roman boy who had been sold into slavery from an aristocratic family, worse than coming into slavery by being taken prisoner, as most were.

"I saw him somewhere – yes, he's here. He wouldn't be with the women. All the centurions have brought slaves – he's with them somewhere."

Stuf spoke with the satisfaction of one who was beholden to no one. He despised those who joined the army, yet he had lived a harder life than any soldier.

Minna felt she was lucky beyond counting that she had landed, literally, in his lap. With him at her side she could outstare the jealous women. How they would be gossiping! All the same she felt uneasy, leaving everything she knew for such an uncertain future, every step taking her irrevocably farther from her home turf and her dear mother in Othona. The slaves had no choice; they were forced to go, but she had her own free will. Was she crazy, as they all no doubt thought? She walked with her head down, trying to come to terms with her decision. There was a possibility, she realized, that Theo would order her home when he found out, probably with an escort to make sure she went. How long before he found out? Not long at all was her guess, with the gossip from the women to their men. By morning he would know.

And then?

II

The army halted at sundown on cleared land beside a river some twenty miles from Camulodunum. It had been an easy march on the hard surface of a well-built road, Stane Street, and word had it that subsequent days could be much harder. The soldiers went into their well-practiced drill of setting up camp, which meant first making a ditch and stockade to encircle the area where the small town of tented accommodations was then put in place.

Minna wanted desperately to stay with Stuf but she knew it was impossible. He would be with the animal handlers, helping feed and later sleeping with them, and she would have to sleep with the other women. There were about twenty of them, a rough and hardened group, mostly wives and slaves of the six centurions commanding the men, and of the older soldiers. As long as the women did not interfere with their men at work they were tolerated. And no army was to be found anywhere without its attendance of hopeful, ragged, homeless women who made themselves useful in exchange for a meal. They all knew Minna, for she had worked in the tribune's house, a servant of high standing – apart from which she was well-known as "the commander's favorite." They endowed this phrase with a meaning that Minna was powerless to contradict. Yes, she was his friend and had been from childhood, but not the way their sneering looks suggested. She told herself that they were jealous, which was true, but it did not help her to feel confident when she went to join them.

They had set up a camp of their own in the far corner of the stockade, using the now empty tent wagon as a base. They had a fire going before the soldiers had finished pitching their tents and were already heating up wine and water and passing around their stock of honey cakes, laughing, complaining, gossiping, while they waited for the supper which would come from the army kitchen. None of them acknowledged Minna as she approached them, although most of them stared with hostile faces and some nudged and whispered and giggled. Minna knew she had to join them, but it sickened her to feel that this was now her place: a camp follower. Theo had not invited her. He was going to be angry with her, she knew, and she dreaded seeing him.

"No room in his tent, then?" one of them sneered.

Minna sat down outside the circle, saying nothing. She wasn't going to argue. If the food came around – and she was starving hungry – she would get her share. That would be sufficient. After that she would sleep under the stars, alone. She had no blanket, nothing but the tunic and thin cloak she stood up in – what on earth had she been thinking of to make this crazy decision? But, her spirits at rock bottom, she refused to regret it. She sat with her knees pulled up, her arms around them, staring into the fire, thinking how close she was to her friends: Theo and Benoc and Stuf and her brother Cerdic and his dog Fortis, even to Draco, son of Cintus, whom Theo had killed –

and yet how alone! Never had she felt so bereft.

One of the women, sitting with her back to her, turned and passed her a cup of the brew they were warming over the fire. She said nothing, just passed the beaker. It was Occa. Minna took the mug gratefully, cupping her hands around its warmth, her mood lightening fractionally. They would get used to her in time, she told herself. The drink made her feel better and the supper, when it came, more so, even if it was only stale bread spread thick with pork grease and a lump of hard cheese.

The camp was now in order, the tents – eight men to each – in exact parallel lines. The commander's tent was in the middle, surrounded by the officers' tents; the busy cookhouse in one corner, where food was already being prepared for the next day. The site was not near any habitation and well clear of forest, just off the road and well-served by a river of crystal clear water. There were signs that it had been used as a temporary camp before. No doubt many armies had passed this way in the last two hundred years, and the same scene of activity, the shouting and laughter, the lowing of oxen and whinnying of horses, the firefly lights of the soldiers' fires sparkling in the darkness had been seen many times by nervous animals lurking in the forest.

It was a cold, clear night, the woodsmoke rising up straight. There were no clouds and the sky was milky with stars, a sure sign of frost now that summer had passed. Minna, in only the thin tunic and light cloak she stood up in, knew she must find something to keep her warm. Stuf would help her. She went to find him where he was preparing to bed down with the oxen, using the great beasts' warm bodies to keep him comfortable.

"I know I can't sleep here," she said, "but I need something to keep me warm. Did you bring anything I can use? It's going to freeze tonight."

"I daresay I can find you something. Has Theo sent for you yet? To bawl you out, send you home?"

"No!"

"He knows you're here."

"How do you know that?"

"I've seen Benoc. He told me."

"Oh, by the gods, is he angry?"

"Benoc said he laughed. Why don't you go to him? Admit all."

"Oh!" Minna felt a rush of joy. "He laughed?" That

was in keeping, why she loved him so. He was never one to stand on ceremony, only when it was to his advantage. He *laughed* to know she was still with him!

But she couldn't go to him, not with his centurions around him and the guard on his tent. It was too public. He was on duty, in a world apart.

"I can't!"

"Go back to your women then, and I will find you some bedding."

Minna went back, nursing her secret joy that Theo had not been angry to know she had followed him. However unfriendly the women, she would not be downcast.

But now they were fed and had drunk some more wine and built up their fire, the women were in a better humor and they made room for her reluctantly. Her presence had been accepted. Stuf came shortly and threw her a warm soldier's cloak and a thick sheep's fleece. She knew better than to ask him how he had come by them. The women all chortled to see such riches.

"You're well provided for! Who's your boyfriend?"

Stuf came from Othona and the women from

Camulodunum did not know him. Better that she passed him off as her boyfriend and they forgot her link with Theo.

She smiled and said nothing.

They had the empty tent wagon and were going to make their beds in it and under it. Minna put her fleece down, wrapped herself in the thick cloak (what soldier was searching for his lost cloak, she wondered, as he prepared for bed?) and lay down on the edge of the shelter. The women were all soon snoring and muttering beside her, but she did not sleep, her mind too heavy with the day's events. She kept thinking of her mother at Othona, and how every footstep was taking her farther and farther away from her, probably forever. Her mother would go on thinking she was safe in Camulodunum and perhaps it was best she didn't know otherwise. Minna knew her wild ways drove her mother to despair but she couldn't help it. She loved her mother, but her mother wanted to tie her in marriage to that oaf Esca, so how could she wonder that her daughter ran away? Minna felt she had a right to arrange her own life, whatever the custom of a child marrying to suit her parents' plans. The irrevocable parting from her mother, though, hung heavily in her mind and she could not sleep. Gradually the camp grew silent around her and the flickers of the little fires sank and died.

Minna sat up, shivering. She thought suddenly of her dear horse Silva, tied up in the horse lines quite close to her. Many times she had slept in the stables at Silva's side and surely now, both of them in a strange place, they would find comfort together? No sooner had the idea entered her mind than she was up and, clutching her precious fleece and cloak, creeping silently towards the horse lines. Silva, the only gray, was easy to spot, lying beside his companion Caractacus, Theo's horse. When he saw Minna he whickered a pleased welcome through his nostrils, but made no move to get up, so completely trusting of the girl who had cared for him all his life.

All Minna's doubts and miseries slipped away as she dropped down beside the gray stallion. Silva turned his head and pushed his muzzle at her as she leaned her cheek on his warm, hard neck. She could not have parted from Silva! He was part of her life; he owed his life to her and loved her as she loved him. She had heard that he was to be used for scouting purposes, ahead of the march, along with Caractacus, but who the scout riders were she did not know. They had to be sharp and brave; Draco, the rider of Caractacus before he joined the army, could well be one of them, or Theo himself might do his own scouting.

Laying her fleece down beside the horse, she wrapped the cloak around her once more and lay hard against Silva's warm back. Now all her worries faded and she felt calm again and satisfied with her judgement. She was right to come. Whatever the future held, it was full of excitement, not like the life of a lady's maid in Camulodunum.

Perhaps she dozed, but she came awake in an instant when she heard a familiar voice softly beside her: "I guessed I'd find you here."

"Oh!"

She could scarcely believe it! She made to scramble to her feet, but Theo laid a hand on her arm and said, "Hush, stay where you are."

In the darkness she saw his silhouette against the starry sky. Then he slipped down and sat beside her, leaning against Silva's back. He was in full uniform – she could tell by the creak of leather and clink of metal – and he smelled of leather and sweat, not as usual of the sweet perfumes of the bathhouse. Those days were over.

"I'm glad you came, Minna, although I shouldn't be. I'm on duty, doing my last round of the camp to see all is in order. So I came to see that you were all in order too. If there's anything you need…"

"No. Stuf got me this cloak and fleece…"

"Stole them from my army, no doubt? Those are rough women you're traveling with. You won't find it easy, Minna, you know that? And I can't help you much. It's more than my position's worth to show you favors."

"I don't want favors."

"No, you never did. I respect that. You know how it is between us, nothing changes. It will never change."

But she didn't know how it was between them, nor ever had. Only how it was for herself. But Theo…he was six years older than she, old enough easily for women. He had been about to marry Julia early in the year when he was being prevailed upon to leave the army and become a government official, but Julia had opted out of it. Theo had been glad. There had been no love there, only politics by their elders. How Minna's heart had leaped at the unraveling of the wedding plans! She knew Theo didn't want marriage, still less to be a pen-pusher. He was wedded to ambition, his army, the prospect of battle. She was just a comfort to him, reminding him of the happy days of their childhood, like a child's toy to rest his cheek against when he had nothing better to do. He was sure of her devotion; she scarcely bothered to hide it these days. Yet she only had to see him, as now, tracing the line of his proud, arrogant nose against the stars, sensing the glint in his night-dark eyes: it took all her will to stay calm and quiet and not make a fool of herself.

"Are you angry at my coming?" she asked. "You took everything: my brother, Fortis, Benoc, Draco, Stuf...Silva. You must have known, when you took Silva... I couldn't stay in Tiberius's house being a maid. When I saw you go, and Silva and Caractacus, I just ran. I couldn't help myself."

"Yes. You belong with us. For now. But later...who knows? I have been given a duty before we go to Caledonia, to settle some scores in the country beyond Derventio. It's not to my liking, but ordered by the Senate of Rome, to make life comfortable for their fat, rich friends who have built villas up there and are being threatened by a maverick gang of Brigantes who have come down from the north. They are fighting over mineral rights, wealth in other words. What else? If we are successful there, we are free to march on. If not..." He shrugged. "Only the gods know that."

Even if it wasn't to his liking, he did not seem reluctant at the prospect. He laughed, yawned, stretched.

"Were you asleep? I must get back. I told Benoc to wait up. Poor Benoc – how he hates this life! I gave him the option to stay in Othona, but he refused it. He said I would need him when I get cut up in battle – well, that's true, should it happen, but I haven't his gloomy outlook. He's a homebody; he likes his comforts. Bathing in the river in the morning will not be to his liking, I can see."

Minna didn't think it would be to anyone's liking, including hers, but the soldiers were hardened through training to extreme discomfort, unlike the household slaves. Their discomfort was of another kind, mainly beatings and kicks and humiliation. Poor Benoc was used to underfloor heating in the commander's villa. Waiting up for Theo in the cold tent would be a miserable chore.

"You must be kind to him. He would die for you."

"I value him, yes. I would not be without him."

Benoc was a couple of years older than Minna, a slender Roman boy with dark, Egyptian eyes like Theo and the same golden dark skin, although not so Arab-looking. They were both far from their roots, unlike Celtic Minna, and the hot sands of the Mediterranean were a distant memory to them, here on the freezing marsh beside the river. No wonder Theo sighed.

"You have what you want," Minna reminded him.

"Yes, in spite of everything. But I still have a black mark beside my name for having defied Tiberius, and I have to redeem myself. I think this chore in the hills beyond Derventio is to try me. These errant Brigantes have a leader, as slippery as an eel, who must be brought to book, they say. If I am successful, I can continue on my way to the wall and I shall get promotion. If not – well, who knows, my little Minna? What then? Disgrace. Back to tax-gathering, counting the sacks of grain in the granary."

He did not sound too upset by the thought, obviously confident that he would not fail. Minna knew he thrived on challenge. He was not a cautious man. She loved his fearlessness.

"I thought you might order me to go home."

"I ought to, yes. There's real danger ahead of us, after all. But I know you're made for better things than curling Julia's hair. I shall see you're safe. And Benoc tells me you're with Stuf – there's no better man than Stuf. So stay, Minna. I'm glad you're here."

He got up and Minna scrambled to her feet too.

"I'll tell Benoc to keep an eye on you. If there's anything you want, tell him. I won't see you again for a while."

And in the darkness he put his arm around her shoulders and gave her a quick hug, pressing her cold body into his smelly armor.

And then he was gone.

III

The march north was tough for the army's train of slaves and servants and women, most of them unused – unlike the army itself – to such hardship. Some of them slunk away back home (although not the slaves, who would face death if recaptured). It crossed Minna's mind to defect once or twice, usually when bathing in an ice-cold river in a private place away from the soldiers. Or when the evening meal did not stretch to the servants, who had to make do with a lump of stale bread only, not even any cheese – that made her remember the delicious titbits the servants used to eat after clearing the tribune's dinner table: the little honey cakes, and the apricots and pears steeped in wine and honey, and sugared almonds and crystallized fruits… But on such a night Stuf would come and whisper to her, "Come to my fire. I've caught a fish. There's enough for both of us." Or he had a rabbit cooking in a hay box in the back of the luggage cart, or some eggs he had found under a hen in passing, or even the hen itself… Stuf knew how to live off the land, having done so all his life.

Sometimes Benoc would bring her a sweetmeat from Theo's table. He would come to Stuf's little fire and huddle close and say, "I don't know how you can stand this. If I were a free man, I would go back."

"What, and leave Theo?" Minna was shocked.

And then Benoc would smile and say, "No. In truth I could never leave him. You know that."

"You go back and I will be his slave," Minna murmured.

"I think you are already," Stuf said cheerfully.

"Poor man, if you looked after him," Benoc said.

Minna was aware that she had no real part in this traveling circus, neither wife nor servant, soldier nor slave. It was only Theo's acknowledged protection of her that gave her status, and Theo was careful not to push the boundary of this fragile relationship. The women now accepted her, and older, tough Occa had shown her friendship in a motherly way, but it was with Stuf and Benoc that she felt at home. Her brother Cerdic sometimes sought her out, but he was becoming rougher and more soldierly by the day and she felt now that she had little in common with him. She liked Draco more, the young native boy whom Theo had taken under his wing after killing his terrible father. Draco loved the horse Caractacus as she loved Silva, and it was in the horse lines that she sometimes met Draco. Unbelievably, the rough, brave, insolent boy Draco had turned into a smart and exemplary soldier. It was he who was given the job of scouting, on Caractacus, and it was Theo who often accompanied him on Silva if the way ahead was dubious and possibly dangerous. If not Theo, Titus, his second-in-command, went scouting on Silva. It was a job Minna longed to do and Benoc actually told her that Theo thought she would be as good at it as any soldier. She had eyes like a hawk and a sure eye for the country.

"Pity you're a girl," Benoc said, laughing, "or Theo would have you in his bodyguard."

Benoc had grown up suddenly, Minna thought – perhaps because his job was now harder, out of a warm villa. In the fort he had been mainly of service to Theo in the bathhouse or at table or keeping his clothes and gear in order – woman's work, in effect – but now he was keeping Theo clean and comfortable in far more difficult circumstances. Theo could be demanding, Minna knew, but Benoc was in no position to question, refuse, or answer back. He was the same age as Stuf, but the two were completely different. Benoc, the slave, was a cultured, graceful, sharp-brained Roman, whereas Stuf was a native Celt, animal-like in his understanding of the land, its wildlife and bounty, bluff and quick with a strong, stocky figure, pale green-blue eyes that missed nothing and tousled brown hair. He could no more have waited on Theo than Benoc could have snared and skinned a rabbit. He was clever enough, had picked up enough Latin to get by on, but had no learning. Nor had Minna, but she was more aware of her lack than Stuf. Stuf didn't care. His nature was gloriously optimistic. Minna had never seen him down. She realized that she was depending on his cheerful presence more and more.

"If one day we ever come to a nice enough place, I'm going to steal off and settle somewhere," he said. "I'm happy to travel with the army so far, but I don't want to meet those Northern thugs that Theo is so anxious to do battle with."

Minna had tried not to think of what lay ahead. From the stories she had heard of life on the wall, she did not relish that future either. Even now, two hundred years after Hadrian had built his amazing wall, in spite of its strong forts and barracks and comforts – even bathhouses! – the incursions from Caledonia never gave the Roman army any peace. The men from Caledonia were animals, so it was said, continually collecting large contingents to try and break through into the south. If Theo wanted action, he was going to the right place. Minna didn't like to think that far ahead.

They marched north along good roads until they came to a legionary fort at a place called Derventio, where Theo received his orders. He was to travel across country to an abandoned fort called Navio which had been taken over by a maverick offshoot of the Brigante tribe from the north. The fort had fallen into disrepair and Theo's orders were to evict the troublemakers and reinstate it, after which he would be relieved and allowed to continue north.

"Or so they say," Theo said doubtfully. But the promise of a bloodthirsty British tribe to annihilate in the near future seemed to make him very happy. The stay at the fort at Derventio meant real comfort for them all for a few days, including the use of the bathhouse. Even the ladies of the baggage train were allowed there for a couple of hours in the morning. The luxury cheered them all, even if the imminent future was grim. The smell of good roasting meat and the laughter from the groups of men drinking and playing dice was a tonic after the hard days on the road. Theo himself came down one evening to address the women's camp. They all stood respectfully, nervous of his presence, as he appeared in the firelight. Minna felt her blood coursing faster as she recognized him, but his eyes did not search for her; rather they looked for the older women, the wives of his soldiers.

"I want to say to you, if you wish, you may stay here when we march on. The fort here will support you, those of you who would prefer it. We have a dangerous task ahead and there will be no place for women. If you come with us, you will have to camp well behind the lines with very little support, in difficult country, looking after yourselves. When our task is done, we will – the gods willing – march on, and contact will be made with you if you stay here, to join us again. It is your choice, to come, or stay. We are going into great danger. I have to warn you."

He stood waiting, as his words sank in.

Occa answered him: "I cannot speak for the others, but I will accompany my man. I think you will find some will want to come, whatever the hardship."

"Yes, I expected that. But the choice to stay safe is available. You can decide amongst yourselves. There is no road ahead, to where we are going. The traveling will be difficult, you must know this. You must be strong to come with us. Let me know the answers in the morning and I will make provision."

He turned away and disappeared into the darkness and a great chattering broke out amongst the women. It was obvious that several of them, the younger ones, thought that staying in the fort with its comforts and settled soldiery was far more appealing than meeting the barbarians in the wilder regions of the north.

Minna told Stuf of Theo's warning.

"Well, he's got enough on his hands without having a load of women to look after," Stuf replied. "These natives have a fierce reputation, and at the moment they're led by a madman called Kimbelinus. The people here say he's taken over the Navio fort. They've tried to take it back but got badly beaten. Their commander here is a weak man, ready for retirement and he won't try again without reinforcements. Now he says he'll back up Theo, but Theo must go in first. So that's the plan. We march to Navio as near as we can without their scenting us, then go in fast – hopefully surprising them."

"We?" Minna questioned. "Have you joined the army after all?"

Stuf grinned.

"I'm unofficial, but Theo wants to use me as a scout. He says if I can steal a joint of meat from the army cookhouse without being seen – which he knows I can – I can put my skills to something useful – spy on the fort without being seen."

"I thought that was Draco's job?"

"Draco goes too. He rides, to get the news back fast, but goes in brigand's gear. He speaks the lingo like a native – which he is, of course – no one will connect him with the Roman army. My job is to see if there are lookouts on the hilltops who might give warning of the army's approach."

Minna was stirred by this news and felt an overwhelming stab of jealousy; while she stayed in camp, the boys were creeping around being spies for Theo, facing real danger and being forced to use all their skills and courage, knowing the success of the army's assault depended on them. By all the gods, if only she were a boy! No wonder Stuf's usual calm demeanor had changed into excitement.

"You're glad you came! You want to do this, don't you? You'll be joining the army before you're through!"

"No. I'm only doing what nature has made me good at. I'm no good at killing. I would never kill. Soldiering is not for me."

Minna realized that Theo's plans were laid and was not surprised to be told they were setting off the next day. The way was now through forest and over rough land, by peasants' ways and animal tracks, far from Roman civilization, and the going would be slow and difficult. Only a hard core of the women elected to follow: Occa and Minna, and a handful of wives, and the slaves who had no choice.

The weather was now cold and wet. The proud lines of the cohort could no longer march in army fashion but had to straggle, often in single file, through overgrown ways. Paths had to be cleared for the baggage wagons; progress was slow. But Theo, by the use of guides from the fort and by riding forward himself to find the best way, made good mileage. Through the hardship a greater sense of camaraderie prevailed, so that in the evening the officers mixed more with the men, and the women were invited to eat by the kitchen and get the best of the fare instead of the leavings. Big fires warmed them and dried their clothes. The wilder the country, the cozier became their camps. They were far from any towns and came across few signs of life. But ahead strange hills could be seen on the horizon, higher than anyone from the south had ever imagined, and no one knew what lay beyond.

IV

After a week's march they stopped in a narrow valley with high crags on either side. Word went around that they were now getting near striking distance of Navio; the fires were to be kept small, voices quiet. Lookouts were posted on the top of the crags and Theo discussed plans with his centurions in his tent. There was a distinct air of nervous tension amongst the men as they clustered around the fires with their platters of bread, cheese and bacon, not sure how many more meals would be coming their way. Stuf was on a high of anticipation, waiting to start his scout duty.

Minna joined him when she had collected her food.

"I've been thinking…" she said. "Benoc said that Theo thought I would be as good a scout as Draco. Why can't I go too, with you and Draco?"

"Because you're a girl."

"Because I'm a girl, no one would suspect we had anything to do with an army. If I were with you, if anyone saw us, they wouldn't give us a thought."

"That's true. But there's no one to see us up here. The countryside's empty."

"Yes, it is here. But as we get closer to Navio it won't be, will it? And the closer we can get without being suspected, the more we can report back."

"Well, you've got a good point. But Theo will never allow you to go."

"I can ask him."

"I dare you!"

Minna had thought up her plan soon after she had heard what the two boys were going to do, and the more she had considered it, the more she was determined to persuade Theo to allow her. She had proved in the past she was as courageous as any boy. Theo knew it and loved her for it. How could he stop her?

She gobbled up her meal and stood up.

"I'm going to ask him."

"He won't let you. Why bother?"

"Come with me."

Stuf shrugged, and got up reluctantly. It took courage to face the commander without good cause.

"Don't tell him this was my idea, whatever you do!"

"No. He will know it's mine."

The night was very cold, the sky full of stars. An almost full moon shone eerily above the strange, high horizon, its austere light seeming to mock the little flickering fires dotted below. The forest pressed in; only an animal track passed through the high crags on either side. No doubt the best path kept to the high ground, out in the open, but that was not where Theo wanted his army. To surprise the enemy was his intention. In his tent his centurions were gathered, discussing the possibilities. They sat around a roughly constructed table, drinking, Theo at its head. Torchlight played on his face, gilding his skin. His cheeks and chin were dark with two days' beard and his cropped hair was longer than usual, curling tightly over his brow. The livid scar above his eye from Cintus's sword gave him a sinister appearance; Minna had not seen him without his helmet for several days. Her breath stuck in her throat at being so close to him, frightened now at her presumption.

Benoc saw her and straightened up from pouring the wine. He said something to Theo and Theo turned and saw her in the doorway of the tent. The other men looked around and the conversation stopped suddenly.

"Why, Minna, have you some news for me?"

Theo's voice was kindly enough, but Minna could see that he was not pleased to see her. She had never broached him in his work before. But she decided that this was, indeed, work.

"Stuf has told me that he and Draco are going to scout for you when we get near Navio. I want to go with them. If I go with Draco and we are seen, no one will connect us with an army, not if Draco has a girl with him. I have better eyesight than either of the boys, and I can ride as well as Draco, and you know I can do this sort of job – I've proved it, you know I have. I want to go. I am asking permission."

Her bravado was received with some astonishment. Some of the men laughed. Theo looked angry.

"Of course you will not go," he said.

"Why do you refuse me?"

"It is too dangerous."

"It doesn't matter. I have faced more danger than this. You know I have."

"The Roman army doesn't employ girls in the fighting line."

"That's why it's a good idea. They will never suspect."

Theo did not reply. Minna saw his mouth tighten in a way that boded trouble – she knew him well enough. She bit her lip angrily. But as she opened her mouth to make another plea, one of the centurions said, "The girl has a point."

Another said, "Does the danger matter? She's answerable to no one. She's only a slave. She's expendable."

"I am not a slave!" Minna cried out.

"And she's not expendable," Theo said savagely. "Not to me."

That he could make this statement publicly before his centurions took Minna's breath away. But she could see he was hardly pleased with her, having forced such a confession, and now had to backtrack. As if to contradict what he had just so rashly stated, he said, "If it were not so dangerous, the idea has substance, I agree."

"We are told that there's a vicus by the old fort where they could buy food, wander around, like any travelers passing by. No one would connect them with an attack," said Titus.

"And they could get a good look at the fort and how it is defended – if it is defended at all."

Minna could see that her idea was being taken up with some enthusiasm. None of the centurions cared a bit for the danger she might put herself in. Only Theo. And Theo could not ignore his men's enthusiasm – he could see that he was the only one with reservations.

"Draco would look after me," Minna said to him quietly. "You trust Draco."

"Yes, I trust Draco."

But his voice was heavy. He gave Minna a wry smile and said softly, "I might have known…bringing you along was a mistake! You court danger."

"Like you," Minna said.

"It's my job. It's not yours."

He looked up then and spoke sharply to one of the men. "Bring Draco here."

Orders were relayed outside and shortly Draco

appeared in the doorway. He was roughly pushed before Theo and straightened himself to attention.

"Sir?"

Theo smiled, amused by the likely reaction Draco would show at finding he was to share his task with a *girl*.

"You start tomorrow, at dawn. Minna goes with you, and take the mare Pesrut."

Draco scowled, appalled. "Minna? I go alone!"

"We think you will be less suspect with a girl in tow. You'll look poor, bedraggled. No one will see you as a Roman soldier spying – that's the point. You can prepare a story to recite – where you're going and why. I leave that to you. With luck you'll go unremarked and no one will question you. We want the layout of the fort and its defenses, and numbers. And anything in the lie of the land that might impede us. Stuf will find out if there are lookouts on the tops that might give warning of our advance, and we will kill them as we go. Have you any questions?"

"The mare, Pesrut...I want Caractacus."

"Caractacus is mine, Draco. Or didn't you notice that I nearly got myself killed acquiring him? Have you forgotten?" Theo was half-angry, half-amused.

"He answers to me."

"And you answer to me. No one will notice you on Pesrut. On Caractacus you will likely be pulled off and left for dead and the horse taken." Theo turned to the men who had brought Draco to him. "Get him stripped of his uniform and find some brigand's dress – a skin, dirty breeches, whatever. A hood of some sort, for his hair is army cropped." Then to Draco he said fiercely, "What you *want*, Draco, is of no importance. What you *do* is for me to say. I won't be questioned."

Draco stared at him insolently, but said nothing. And Theo smiled and said softly, "I chose you for this job, Draco. It's of prime importance. You should be proud."

Draco dropped his eyes. "Yes, sir."

As he left the tent he shot Minna a baleful look. Stuf came up close to Minna, grinning, and said, "You'd be better off with me, I think. He'll be a sweet traveling companion."

Minna, now she realized she was successful in her crazy ambition to see some excitement, suddenly no longer felt as brave as she had when the idea had first come into her head. She hadn't expected such instant gratification. She could see now that Theo was angry with her. He shouted at Benoc to bring some more wine and dismissed Stuf with a curt, "I'll talk to you before you leave in the morning." The centurions left too, with Draco.

Minna was left alone with Theo in the shadowy tent where the small oil lamp flickered fretfully on the table. It was stone-cold, bleak, far from the comforts of their home fort. The high crags on either side of their cramped site seemed to press down, darker against dark. Through the door flap the line of them shut out the stars, shut out life, Minna thought with a shiver. What was she doing?...When she could have stayed behind as a favored servant in calm Camulodunum, where the villa was safe and warm, the food sweet, her mistress kind.

Theo gestured to her to sit at the table and Benoc silently handed her a vessel and poured wine. He was completely expressionless, yet she knew he would be loving this drama. Benoc missed nothing.

"Get out," Theo hissed at him.

Benoc put the amphora down and went and stood outside the tent, to wait. Thank the gods, Minna thought, I am not a slave.

"So, you stupid child, how can I protect you when

you put your crazy ideas before my men? Do you never stop and think?" Theo turned on Minna angrily. "They don't care about your going into danger, they don't care if you get captured and tortured."

His voice dropped: "It just so happens that I do. I love your spirit; I can't help it."

Minna could not see his expression, the lamp so feeble, but there was a tremor in his voice.

"I wanted you to come on this journey, Minna, I love to know you are there, even if I scarcely see you. The thought of you gives me courage, and I need it, the gods know it – I have never led men in battle before...it matters terribly that I succeed here. It should be easy with so well-trained a force, but these barbarians are on their home ground and their leader, Kimbelinus, has a fearsome reputation."

Minna had heard this gossip from Stuf. The name Kimbelinus had reached afar; they had first heard the man mentioned back in Derventio.

"It's Kimbelinus who has taken over the Navio fort?"

"Yes. And we need to know how strongly it is held and how protected so that we are prepared. Perhaps you will bring good news back – that they are lax and scarcely armed, that they drink a lot, that their defenses are poor…perhaps not. A great deal depends on your scouting. Draco's scouting, that is. I would like to forbid you to go but if I do my men will laugh at me. They think I love you – you, a scrap of a girl, when I could have married Julia, who would have made my career path easy. But I shall never marry. We've spoken of this before. What is between us is something only you and I understand."

Minna thought the wine was speaking. But she trembled all the same. She could not think of anything to say to him. He stood up and came to her side.

"May the gods protect you tomorrow."

He put his arm around her and gave her a quick hug. She buried her face momentarily in the inhospitable front of his leather uniform. The metal epaulettes repelled her cold cheek, the soldier smell of sweat and leather filled her nostrils, and she straightened up sadly, finding no comfort. Benoc was watching from the doorway. She shook her hair back and, scowling, went out into the dark night. She was shaken by what had happened, and what had been said. What was between herself and Theo was something she found hard to understand, even if Theo acknowledged it. It left her in limbo, unable to relate to any other man. Once she thought she could love the dashing Draco or even kindly, clever Stuf if she were free to love, but it wasn't possible while Theo was there. But what did she expect, when she had been so sure to follow him? He hadn't invited her, after all.

She blundered back through the tents towards the women's place. As she passed the horse lines she stopped by force of habit to say goodnight to Silva. Pressing her face into his soft mane, she thought how much easier it was to love a horse, the love returned without question, the comfort a blessing.

V

Draco was not an agreeable companion; resentment oozed from his body as he and Minna rode away from the camp. Pesrut was a small horse and Minna was forced to press herself against Draco's back whether she wanted to or not. His anger was transmitted: she could feel it, boiling beneath his rough cloak. It made her angry too, but there was nothing she could say. She understood his pride and independence. Perhaps they would be more convincing as a quarreling couple, passing through strange country? At least his angry back kept her warm.

It was just breaking dawn, late at this time of year in the gray and cold winter. Once away from the camp the country seemed completely hostile, the forest bearing down on them, the sky low and forbidding, shedding raindrop tears. Somewhere above the forest, Stuf was already on his way, making for the crest of the high ground where lookouts were likely to be posted. He had more ground to cover than they did, if he was to check both sides of the valley. As Pesrut jogged on her way, the valley was opening out. The high crags fell away, the trees thinned and, in the growing light, a wide and fertile valley ran before them. Beyond the valley, far in the distance, a line of hills blocked the way. They were incredibly high, almost like a wall, and, with a faint, pearly shaft of sunlight slanting across their tops from the east, they made as beautiful a sight as Minna had ever seen. Almost like the sea, she thought, in their aloof disdain of the little ants that were the human beings who ran around on its shores. These hills were not to be tamed, she felt sure. There was no sea here, but the mountains instead spoke of the might of the gods. Minna shivered. The grandeur of sea and earth crushed human pretensions.

"Have you ever seen land like that before?" she muttered in Draco's ear.

He did not answer. She knew he hadn't. But he was too proud to admit to not knowing anything.

She had no idea what to expect when they reached their destination, but as Pesrut continued at her gliding jog-trot (she had always been a popular mount because of her smooth paces) and came steadily down the valley, the path beneath her hooves became more marked. Trees and scrub were cut back, and here and there on the hillside one or two rough dwellings surrounded by small areas of cultivated land were visible. Thin skeins of smoke blew from their roofs. They were coming to the edge of a center of habitation, planted where the valley they were following from the south met the large valley that ran east to west beneath the shadow of the mountain ridge. Minna could see why a fort would have been built in this place, commanding a crossing of roads and a convergence of rivers. It was an obvious travelers' route. The fort was here, according to Theo, but in front of it was a sprawling habitation where the usual native population had moved in to profit from the former Roman presence. As they came down past the last fold in the hills, the place was revealed to them. Draco halted Pesrut and they stood taking in the place they had come to spy on.

It was by now mid-morning, gray and cold. Woodsmoke from the myriad fires swirled in the air, and with it came the smell of meat cooking, the sound of iron being hammered on an anvil, the bleating of sheep in the butcher's pen...it was all perfectly familiar. Just like home, Minna thought optimistically. They could go and buy some bread and meat just as they would have done back at Othona or Camulodunum. Then look around.

Draco said to her, "You're to keep quiet. Your voice is too like a Roman's. I'll do the talking."

His voice was still as broadly Celtic as it had always been. He looked the part, too, in the old skins the soldiers had found him and the mothy scarf tied around his head. Minna knew she didn't look any smarter and Pesrut was no better than some of the ponies that grazed behind the huts. The centurions had given them a few bits and pieces to barter with: some beads and a silver clasp, a bag of raisins, a leather dog collar. The few coins they had were the most common, much rubbed, nothing shiny from the latest minting in Londinium. Minna knew that if the two of them had been approaching Camulodunum, no one would have given them a second glance. But in this smaller place strangers might not be overlooked. So her heart beat nervously as Draco nudged Pesrut on towards the first outlying huts.

"We'll just go straight through," Draco growled at her. "The fort is supposed to be on the left of the road, on the high ground above the river."

The first people they met, a farmer driving geese with a boy and a dog, merely gave them a rude stare and a woman coming the same way with a basket of eggs on her arm nodded without a smile, not interested. Minna felt her jumping nerves relax. They rode on between the usual roughly-built workshops and homes and the tethered oxen and milking cows and found nothing more than a poor run-down village. If it had once relied for its living on a Roman fort it showed no signs of it now. The people were shabby and morose, taking no interest in them, too busy haggling over the poor wares on show, or gossiping in the wine shop. Pesrut passed down the muddy street unchallenged and Draco did not stop, his eyes on the remains of the army fort that now came into sight on a plateau of high ground above the road. They could see its great walls, broken through in many parts, and the remains of a gateway facing the road, its arch fallen in. Dwellings of timber, reed-hatched, were scattered around it and had been built inside among the ruins of the familiar lines of barracks and stores.

Ruined it might be, but it was obviously now put to good use by what was presumably Kimbelinus's army. For it swarmed with men, a far braver-looking tribe than the farmers down in the village. There seemed to be one or two hundred of them, all at different activities: building, cooking, fighting, lolling around drinking, making a lot of noise and generally giving the impression of being in control and enjoying life.

As they watched, Draco and Minna saw a small group ride out on scruffy ponies. They came down the hill from the gateway, squelching through thick mud, laughing and shouting at each other. They all wore swords, Minna noticed, and looked to her – accustomed as she was to the standards of the Roman army – exceedingly hairy and unkempt. But fierce and strong. If these were the offshoot of the Brigantes, Theo's adversaries, she thought grimly, they were worthy of his respect.

Draco stopped Pesrut and backed her into some trees off the road to keep out of the way, but the men rode past with scarcely a glance, throwing clods of mud all over them. The man at the front was lean and filthy, with white teeth laughing through his grimy beard, very blue eyes sweeping without interest over Pesrut and her riders.

"Kimbelinus himself," Draco said when they were past.

"Kimbelinus! How do you know that's him?"

"I know him. He's kin. My father's cousin."

Minna was stunned.

"Cintus! Kimbelinus is Cintus's cousin?"

Theo had killed Cintus in a sword-fight and taken Draco prisoner and enrolled him in his army. He had been unwilling, born a Roman-hater, but had fallen under Theo's spell. He had realized there was no life for him as a brigand without his father, and life in the Roman army was not unappealing. But his grudge against all that was Rome had not gone away, it was so deeply ingrained.

"When the attack happens, you will be fighting your kin!" Minna said, horrified.

She could not see Draco's expression, riding behind

him, and he did not reply. It seemed to her a terrible situation to be in. Surely he was torn in two halves? She knew he loved and respected Theo, yet the enemy was his own blood, his kin. How could one turn on one's own family?

All Draco said was, "We'll follow them, see what happens below the fort."

The men were well away, almost out of sight. Draco took Pesrut past the fort along the road that went down below the wall with the broken gateway in it. They both took note that the walls were easy to breach, broken down as they were. A lot of the material from the walls seemed to have been used to improve the roadway below, which led to a wide ford across the river. Nearly three hundred years ago, when the fort was built, it must have been a fine defensive building, standing proud over the wide valley beneath the great ridge of the hill crest. Even in ruin it was impressive.

Kimbelinus and his men had gone this way, crossed the ford and were now well away, riding eastward along the main valley. Draco stopped at the ford and decided they should ride in the opposite direction, to make a circle all the way around the fort to see how easy it was to attack from above, instead of through the village. They followed the river, keeping out of sight among the trees. There was nobody there. A few thin pigs foraged, and voices floated down distantly from the fort. It was very still in the woods, windless, cold. The mare's hooves squelched along the peaty path, loosing a scent of long dead leaves, of old bones, Minna thought, of people here long before the Romans came. How far did people go back? Why did the arrogant Romans think they could rule this land, taking it from the likes of Kimbelinus and Draco whose roots were deeper here than ever the Romans' could be? Because they were stronger, more clever, more civilized? But equally as bloodthirsty. Why did men fight and kill all the time? she wondered, seeing in her mind the impending bloodshed in this beautiful countryside. The great ridge of hills revealed itself through gaps in the trees and the sun was shining on its crest and it was serene and glorious, rising clear against the thin gray air. Minna suddenly wanted to be up there, away from the mean acts that she was now a part of. She was really stupid to have thrust herself into this useless role. To impress Theo – had that been her reason? Draco could have done without her.

But her spirits rose as they recrossed the river and

climbed up out of the trees on to a wide hillside on the far side of the fort. Draco rode as close as he dared, but there seemed to be no lookouts or guards – it wasn't an army, after all, just a gang of brigands without discipline making a home. The walls were as tumbled here, merely holding up rows of ill-built shacks. But there seemed to be a large number of men in residence.

"The commander wanted numbers," Draco said. "But it's difficult. How can you tell?"

Minna guessed that Draco couldn't count. In an oblique way he was asking her help. But one could only estimate. Some twenty or so had ridden off with Kimbelinus and there seemed to be at least four times as many in the fort, and who knew how many roaming over the countryside who would come back at night?

"At least a couple of hundred. Not all that many. Tell him two hundred. Our army will beat them easily. We are twice as many, and our men are trained. These men are a rabble."

"They will be outnumbered but they are brave," Draco said. "They will not give in easily. The Romans at Derventio feared them."

They rode on past the fort and kept to a track on the hillside to avoid the vicus they had passed through on their way down. They passed shepherd boys guarding sheep and a few women who ignored them, and were soon able to drop down onto the road they had come in on. The expedition had been completely uneventful. After being so nervous, Minna felt almost cheated, riding back in a thin midday sunlight, bright and cold. Pesrut's flanks warmed her bare legs and a mothy sheepskin Stuf had found her kept the breeze off her back. Draco too had thawed out towards her now the danger was over.

"I suppose Theo will make the attack soon, now you can tell him how the land lies," Minna said (tactfully using "you" instead of "we").

"He wants to get on. Why would he wait around? None of us like waiting around. I expect we'll go tomorrow."

In which supposition he was correct.

VI

When Minna went to fetch a skin bagful of water up from the river in the evening she found her brother's lovely dog Fortis prancing at her side. A fine big tawny-colored wolfhound with strange golden eyes and a great plumy flag of a tail, he knew her as a friend from puppyhood. His mother Mel had lived in the family home before Cerdic joined the army.

"Why, Fortis, you silly old beggar! Where's Cerdic then?"

She knew he couldn't be far away. She had wanted to see him before the battle, in case...her thoughts stopped abruptly there. She had scarcely seen him at all on the march. He was a soldier now, scornful of sisters. Since he had joined the army they had grown apart. But he stood there now, unsmiling.

"I'm leaving Fortis with you. You'll care for him?" No brotherly preamble.

"Of course."

"We go in the morning, early."

"Are you afraid?"

"Yes. Of course."

And Minna saw her old brother standing there, her childhood playmate along with Theo, the companions of her escapades in the old fort at Othona. How happy they had been! And now, the three of them, still together, but completely separated. She felt she had little in common anymore with this gawky, hard-faced soldier, but her heart felt for him, her own flesh and blood. How her mother would be weeping if she could see the pass her children were now in! As if thinking the same things, Cerdic gave Minna a rueful smile.

"Why did I join the army? I often ask myself. Stuf has more sense. You are the first to know I am not brave. I dread battle."

"I doubt you're the only one. Even Theo—"

"I am frightened of betraying him, running away,

screaming even, of not being brave. You know what I am, Minna. I wouldn't say this to anyone else."

Minna suspected he had been drinking, being so maudlin.

"Come on, you're splendidly trained, you have all the advantages against these ruffians. You're not alone this time, Cerdic. Of course you will not fail. Theo is a great man to follow."

"Yes, his tactics are clever. We are well-briefed. They will be taken by surprise if all goes to plan, and it will be over in no time. All the same, pray for me, Minna, and be good to my dog. I trust you utterly."

"You know I will. I will keep Fortis by my side till you come back and I'll be praying all day!"

Cerdic laughed. "We're not very good at prayers! Only if we want something. Here, take the dog's leash, else he'll follow me."

He caught the dog and handed the lead to Minna. Minna took it, and on an impulse threw her arms around him and kissed his cheek.

"Come back safe! You and Theo! I'll pray for you both."

"Goodbye, Minna." He awkwardly removed himself from her hug, turned, and walked smartly away.

*　*　*

The army left silently before dawn and the camp
followers made a forlorn gathering around the cooking
fire to await their return. Minna tried to keep her mind
off the knowledge that Theo was leading the attack.
She tried not to think about it at all, but she noticed
her hands trembled when she poured the water into
the cauldron over the fire. She knew she looked as
wan as the others whose men had gone off to do battle.
No one knew how many would come back; they only
knew that they would be needed then, to bind up
wounds and pound up healing herbs. Occa was the
matriarch who knew all about these concoctions, just
as Minna's mother had, and Minna knew which herbs
to look for without being told. Occa had a huge bag
of clean linen for bindings, and thread sutures for the
surgeons, and strong spirit to daze the amputees.

The fate of the army weighed heavily. Nobody
supposed they would be beaten, but at what price, who
could say? The reputation of the Brigante offshoot was
impressive and it was impossible to think of anything
else. The army had marched off silently into the
darkness, as ceremoniously as if they were on parade,
in spite of the fact that the campsite was fast becoming

a sea of mud. The idea of taking the fort and making a proper place to live in after the weeks since leaving Camulodunum had inspired their cheerful exit.

"They are soldiers after all," Occa said grimly, "and fighting is what they are for. This hanging around does an army no good."

Yes, they liked it, Minna knew. Now, swinging into action, Cerdic's fears would have flown, she was sure. Theo had been laughing, his black eyes shining with excitement, as they slipped away down the road. The men had all been eager, chattering away, until the order came for silence. The attack was to be a surprise, no trumpets, no gleaming standards, but a fast, quiet approach from the side of the hill where the wall was most broken. Draco and Minna had described the place minutely to Theo and his centurions. Minna had been able to draw a plan, and Stuf had pinpointed the few positions where lookouts had been placed: "Mostly asleep, or drunk," he said dismissively.

So now they waited.

There was no sun, just a lowering sky and pinpricks of rain, a thoroughly depressing day, the evening coming early. As the afternoon drew on they were silent, and some walked out a way to perhaps meet a messenger. But Minna went to the horse lines to find comfort with her dear Silva. The horses, thank the gods, were not involved in battle. He stood there quietly beside Theo's horse Caractacus. What a pair they made! Not many of the army horses had the injection of Barbary blood that these two had, the blood from the horses of the Arabian deserts that gave fire and beauty to the produce of the native ponies. The gray and the chestnut, they were both stallions, high-crested, with fine heads and large gentle eyes. Silva's dam, the little native pony Pesrut, stood with them, the pony that had given Silva her own common-sense and intelligence. The mix had resulted in a rare animal; Minna knew Silva was special and grieved that she did not own him. How could she, such a valuable animal, in spite of the fact that it was she who had saved and reared him as a foal? But a home with the army was as good a home as a horse could get and while she was with the army all was well. She took both of them tidbits from the feed bin and some for Pesrut too, and was standing with her cheek snuggled against Silva's warm neck when suddenly Fortis, sitting obediently by her side, stood up, whined, sat down again on his haunches, pointed his nose in the air and started to howl. It was a strange, blood-curdling noise, like that of a hungry wolf.

"What is it? Oh, Fortis, what's wrong? What do you know?"

Minna flung herself down beside him and wrapped her arms around his shaggy shoulders. His big amber-gold eyes in the dusk were full of tears. But dogs didn't cry! Fortis shook her hands away and howled.

"Stop it! Stop it! Oh, Fortis, hush, I can't bear it!"

Then the dog laid his long snout on her shoulder and the howling dropped to a whimper. Minna stroked and hugged him, her blood running cold with what the dog's despair meant. Dogs knew. She knew now that Cerdic, her brother, wasn't coming back, and Fortis was telling her. Fortis knew.

Minna wept.

"Oh, Fortis, it's Cerdic, isn't it?" She buried her face in his damp, smelly coat and her hot tears ran into his fur. Was it for Cerdic? Not for the whole army surely? The dog's body shook with what could only be sobs and he would not move, only shiver and whimper.

As Minna kneeled there crying, Stuf came along to start the feeding.

"What's wrong?"

She told him and knew Stuf would understand. He knew everything about animals and did not dispute the reason for Fortis's distress.

"Don't cry, Minna." He put his arms gently around her shoulders. "If it truly is so, perhaps he has gone to a better life, with the spirits, who knows? Poor Cerdic. He should have stayed with me. He wasn't cut out for the army."

"He wanted it so, but when he was there he didn't like it."

But what had Cerdic liked? He had always been discontented, save when he was with his dear dogs. Perhaps there was something better beyond death, where he would find what he had always been looking for. His old dog Mel, Fortis's mother, had died the previous year. Was she waiting for him, to fawn on him with kisses from her long pink tongue?

"At least the horses didn't have to go into battle," Minna whispered.

Theo's army was too small to boast a cavalry, but a message reached them in the late afternoon that Theo was desperate to have Caractacus; Kimbelinus had gotten away on one of his rough ponies and to give chase on foot was hopeless. The attack was successful;

the fort had been cleared. Theo was unscathed and Roman injuries were small: six killed and few serious injuries. Minna waited with a desperate hope to hear in spite of the dog's knowledge that Cerdic was safe, but Cerdic was, indeed, one of the dead.

Minna's profound relief at Theo's safety was deeply scored by knowing her brother was dead. Love for her faraway mother welled up in her grief; when her mother heard the news her heart would bleed. Minna felt deeply guilty at having left her without word, for now there was no one to comfort her. But Cerdic had always been her favorite. She had spoiled him terribly, which was perhaps why he had been such a discontented boy. But now Minna could only remember the fun they had had as children, when Theo had been their playmate, escaping from the authority of his parents and tutors to swim and play in the mud, cross the marshes, steal boats, take the dogs into the forest to hunt...to get into all sorts of trouble, always led by Theo. The two of them had been Theo's escape. However many beatings he got, Theo had always been ready for more fun. And Cerdic then had laughed all day long, and longed to join the army, always longing for what he couldn't have. When he was a soldier, he was always talking of deserting, in spite of the terrible punishments for doing so. Well, thought Minna, he has deserted now, forever, into the lands of the gods, and the gods grant that he may find the happiness of his childhood again.

The messengers came to tell them to move up to the fort the following morning, when a bodyguard would come to escort them. They none of them slept much that night but sat around the fire talking, relieved and happy that a more permanent home was in sight, at least for a while. If Kimbelinus had gotten away, Theo's task of making the area safe for the Roman bigwigs was not completed. He would make the fort his headquarters and work from there. Nobody thought it likely that a man like Kimbelinus would ride away never to trouble them again. There had to be a more decisive victory.

Minna sat silently with Fortis at her side. The big dog was grieving and would eat nothing. Minna stroked him, unable to take part in what became quite a party, a victory party for the success of the raid. Later she crept away, leaving the celebrations, and went to sleep with Fortis lying beside her, her sheepskins over them both. The big dog kept trembling, yet he was not cold.

"Oh, poor Fortis! I know how you feel."

But Theo was safe! This happy thought kept bursting up through her grief – she was torn in two parts.

The next day an escort of soldiers came to dismantle and load the tented camp and all its equipment onto the wagons and take them to the fort. The journey was the same that Minna had made with Draco, but this time she rode Silva and led Caractacus at the back of the train, and the dejected Fortis followed at their heels. Thank the gods Theo had not taken the horses, even if he had lived to regret it. But she could see already that they would have a part to play in hunting down Kimbelinus.

In spite of the fact that they were the victors, it was not a happy entry into the fort at Navio. It was a still, misty day, quite warm, but the people Minna had seen before bustling in the vicus outside the walls had now withdrawn inside their huts, or fled, and the street was empty save for a few scavenging dogs. As they approached the fort they began to hear the familiar buzz of the soldiers about their business and see figures at work. As they came in sight, more men came to meet them, and soon they had entered the broken walls and all the gear was being unloaded and the tents newly erected on the sites of the old barracks. The soldiers were obviously euphoric with their victory. Minna watched as the women embraced their men, the hard-faced Occa actually in tears in the arms of an old warrior, Gaius.

Forlorn, Minna looked for the laid-out dead, and was led by a young soldier whom she knew was Cerdic's friend to the sad line of corpses lying under the far wall. They were covered with bloodstained cloaks, and the young man peered under the covers until he found Cerdic, and pulled back the cloak to reveal his face.

"There. It was so quick, he didn't suffer. I saw it happen, but I couldn't help him."

"Was he fighting?" Minna asked. She did not dare add, "Or running away?"

"Fighting like a wild boar! He was so brave, trying to stave off two men with swords, and then another came up behind him. He didn't stand a chance."

Minna's heart swelled with pride and love. He had risen to the occasion. Perhaps he had, with his last breath, died happy. His face was the face of a boy asleep. There was nothing horrific there, no sign of wounds, only of peace. He didn't look like a soldier, but just like the boy Minna had played with back at Othona, the darling of his mother. Minna burst into sobs. Fortis crept up and softly licked Cerdic's face.

The boy drew back suddenly and saluted, and Minna saw Theo through her tears and turned to him instinctively.

"Ah, poor Minna! Poor Cerdic!" Theo murmured.

He put his arms around her and held her against his breast. Oh, the warmth and the comfort, the love, how she longed for it! But so brief the moment. She straightened up, ashamed, and drew back. Remembered her place.

"I weep for your brother, Minna. He was my good friend as well as your blood. I would have wished it differently."

But Minna could see that the grief was overridden by the great euphoria of his victory. His first battle, leading his cohort! She wondered then if he had been as frightened as Cerdic in the dark hours before the start; impossible, she thought, not to be. So much honor at stake – for Cerdic it was only his skin.

"You must be proud," she whispered. "Your victory."

"Half a victory. The leaders escaped, so the business is not finished."

"Perhaps they won't come back."

"Yes, they'll come back. Kimbelinus is a proud man. I wounded him. He won't forget. His men saved him, and then I had to save myself. It was a great fight, Minna, but tragic that we had to lose these men."

Minna could see that he was still excited at the memory of it: he had *enjoyed* it!

She stared at him in wonder, at the gleam of satisfaction in his eyes, at the sword slashes in his leather tunic, the dried blood still on his bare arms. She turned away, sickened.

"The men are building a pyre across the river. This afternoon we will give them our blessing and send them into the care of Mithras and a better life. Don't be sad, Minna."

"At least you are safe," she whispered. "I feared for you so."

"Poor Minna! But tonight we will celebrate our victory and you will be happy."

Minna could easily guess how that would turn out, a great drunken debacle under the stars. If Kimbelinus had any sense he would return at dawn when they would all be in a stupor, too drunk to fight. How stupid men were!

But perhaps they deserved the chance to enjoy themselves, for the work to set up a new camp was prodigious, tired as they were after the battle. And Theo ordered them to bathe in the river and turn out clean for the funeral rites, which was not popular. The rites were brief. Minna watched from a distance, holding the shivering Fortis, and withdrew as the men came back into the camp. The women had been allocated a place at the bottom end of the fort, nearest the river, and already they had made camp and lit a fire, but most of them were busy tending to the wounds of the injured. This was obviously going to be an ongoing chore, for some men were already delirious after the attention of the army surgeons, a few not far from death from blood loss. Theo went down to the vicus to try and reassure the hiding people that the army meant them no harm, that they could continue with their lives as before, but he did not meet with great success.

It seemed the people of the village trusted no one; they were glad the aggressive Kimbelinus had been sent packing, but they were Britons, after all, and hated the Romans who had tried to appropriate the area's main source of wealth: the lead and silver mines. Most of them worked in the mines, slaves to a Roman governor who owned a large villa ten miles up the main valley to the west. But Kimbelinus had targeted this mining and caused the Roman governor much grief, having stolen and hidden a large cache of the lead ingots waiting to be transported to Rome, and the mining had come to a halt. At the same time he had not endeared himself to the local population, helping himself to all their foodstuffs and cattle without payment and treating them as badly as had the Romans.

Not unexpectedly, this governor lost no time in sending a messenger to inquire about the battle and demand Theo's presence at his villa. Theo told the messenger his master could wait until their camp in the captured fort was established, the men were comfortable and the injured were out of danger.

"Then tell him I will visit and we can discuss what to do next," he told the messenger.

The messenger looked slightly worried about taking this cavalier reply but departed on his horse into the evening dusk.

"Kimbelinus is not finished with us, I'm sure," Theo said.

He ordered permanent patrols out on the surrounding hillsides to watch for any movement, and no one left the camp save to go to the vicus and arrange for provisions.

Although not loved, the Roman army was received with far more cordiality when the local people realized that the army, unlike Kimbelinus, was willing to pay for meat and corn. Theo, inspired by his hero Julius Caesar, believed in making friends with the conquered.

But the messenger came again to order his presence at his master's villa.

"I will go tomorrow," Theo told him.

When the messenger had gone, he laughed and said to Benoc, "The man is too frightened to leave his villa, so I hear. I will go without a bodyguard and take Minna with me, to show my contempt. I will tell him she's my slave."

"She won't like that," said Benoc.

"She will like it when I tell her she can ride Silva at my side," Theo said. "Go and give her my orders, and see that the horses are properly turned out."

So the next day Minna's dearest wish came true, to ride out with Theo on Caractacus and herself on Silva, the two horses side by side.

VII

The two horses were brought up to Theo's tent from the horse lines. His new headquarters were nearly finished, so hard had the soldiers worked. The barracks were almost completed, but the outer defensive walls remained as heaps of rubble. So many of the stones had been plundered and removed that there was not enough material to rebuild them. There was no evidence to say where all the stones had gone, but Theo was not interested. He did not want a siege battle with Kimbelinus, to be starved out of the fort over a long period of time. He preferred to fight in the open, and without the walls the camp provided a good view over the surrounding countryside. All the filthy debris left in stinking heaps by the barbarians was burned and cleared away.

The horses were groomed to perfection, their winter coats shining in the pale sun, their manes and tails combed far more beautifully than most of the women had managed their own hair.

Theo was equally finely turned out by Benoc, as was Minna by her own efforts, along with a little help from Occa. Bathing in the river was horrible but necessary, and Occa had helped her with her hair, which now gleamed hay-gold in one long braid down her back. If her cloak was soldier's issue, at least it was clean and newish (Stuf had "found" it for her, the evening before). Mounted on her beloved Silva, she was aware that the soldiers seeing them off were amused by Theo taking her as his slave, but they liked the joke and she was not offended. It was wonderful to accompany him; even the element of danger excited her. The bodyguard, disappointed to miss the excursion, admired Theo's effrontery. They knew that the Roman governor who dared not leave his villa would be humiliated by the young commander's confidence. The man's character had preceded him from Derventio; he was said to be rich on other people's toil, greedy, a bully and cruel to his slaves and servants. Two of his servants had already escaped and come to the fort and asked to be enrolled in the army. Theo had set them to building, to see their commitment.

"Come, slave," he said now to Minna, laughing, and vaulted onto Caractacus.

The two stallions reared and cavorted as they rode through the gates, longing for a gallop, but Theo reined Caractacus in and said, "No, Minna, we must arrive cool and collected. We have to impress the gentleman."

Minna rode in a dream of happiness. The ride could not be long enough for her. The road along the main valley was good; the river, full with winter rain from the surrounding hills, burbled and gushed noisily beside them and above, to the north, amazing hills dipped and swung against the sky. Minna, brought up in the gentle, rolling land of Essex, had never seen such mountains, yet they were said to be as nothing compared with what lay farther to the north.

"So where are these lead mines they're fighting over?" she asked Theo.

"They are all around us, mostly small workings.

Some go into the hillside but most are opencast. There are natural caves in this area with seams of silver, and a blue stone which is pretty, but not all that valuable – so I've been told. I'm no expert. It's not what interests me. Settling the score with Kimbelinus is my department. This Julius Aulus Petronius we are about to visit wants him out of the way so that he can take back his mines. I expect he'll be angry that the man got away but I can't help that. I'm not expecting to be embraced like a long-lost son."

"You've taken the fort back. Surely he'll be grateful for that?"

"We'll see."

The villa lay in a bowl of well-tilled land at the end of the valley where hills rose up all around to enfold it. It was a new, expensive-looking domain with extensive outbuildings and animal shelters in a courtyard around it, and with an imposing arched gateway.

"I think I know now where the stones from the fort walls went to," Theo said, pulling up to take in the view. "The blackguard – to steal from his own! He must have an army of slaves to have transported all that material."

It was the first sign they had seen of Roman

domestic occupation since setting out across country from Derventio. It was within striking distance of several forts and garrisons to the northwest, and a good road led from them down to Navio, over the hills. The native people were used to being harassed and moved on by the people they still thought of as the invaders and although many had come to terms with living under Roman rule there were always the firebrands like Kimbelinus who liked to fight for what they considered their land. Men liked fighting, Minna knew: the gods had made them like that. There was little to be done about it.

There were guards on the gate who stopped them peremptorily.

"Theodosius Valerian Aquila, to wait on your master, with his slave." Theo spoke in a loud, scornful voice. The men drew back hastily.

Minna nearly giggled as she slipped off Silva. Theo threw her his reins and said, "Come to me when you've put up the horses," in the same curt tones he used to Benoc, but some boys scurried forward to take the horses so she was able to follow Theo as he entered the house. She walked demurely, eyes down, but inside her heart was leaping with excitement.

The house was very grand in spite of being in such an isolated place, and spoke of great wealth, which no doubt stemmed from the mining. Minna could see quite clearly how angry the native people must be to see their riches creamed off, when they were so poor and beggarly. This Julius was said to treat his workers abominably and he gave them no share of his spoils. She was ready to hate him.

When he appeared from an inner room his appearance did nothing to make her change her mind. He was a big man of about fifty, fleshy and brash, with small piggy eyes full of suspicion and a thin-lipped, tight mouth. He looked Theo up and down as if he were a slave for sale.

Theo came quickly to attention.

"Theodosius Valerian Aquila at your service, sir."

"Hmm."

Julius's eyes traveled sharply over him and then turned on Minna with a leer.

"And this?"

"My slave, sir."

"Really?" He gave a disbelieving sneer. "You can give orders in the kitchen, girl, that refreshment be taken out to your bodyguard." His voice was sharp.

"There is no bodyguard, sir," Theo said. "We came alone, the girl and I."

The man's eyebrows jerked up in surprise.

"You are foolish. You are new here. Don't you know the dangers?"

"I was sent to quell the dangers, sir, not avoid them. We have taken possession of the fort and the rabble in it have retired for the time being. This valley is safe now. I have lookouts posted on the hillsides to give warning of any possible counter-attack."

"Good. Because they will come back, I have no doubt. Kimbelinus got away?"

"Yes, unfortunately."

"He will organize them again. We are not safe until he is killed."

"Or is given back what he thinks is his? A share, at least, to give the natives work?"

An angry flush came into Julius's heavy cheeks.

"Don't talk like a puppy! They work the mines to our orders, and we pay them what they are worth, which is very little. You have no idea…a gang of them under Kimbelinus stole the ingots we were about to transport to Deva, for Rome. They weighed so heavily…we could not believe it possible."

He turned his head and bawled towards the doorway where his slaves were waiting.

"Bring wine, you dogs!"

He gestured to Theo to follow him to a table and chairs, and sank down heavily into one of the cushioned seats.

"Sit, and I will tell you what I will have you do."

Minna, following to stand behind Theo, sensed his indignation at being given orders by this toad. Julius was not his military master, only someone to whom Theo's presence was giving relief. Did he have the authority to tell Theo what to do? Minna thought not. But Julius obviously thought he did.

"We want our stolen ingots recovered. We have searched everywhere we know in the area – they cannot have moved them far. There are caves and potholes everywhere...we have scoured them but to no avail. You must set your army to recovering them. That is your priority. Get one of Kimbelinus's men and squeeze the truth out of him as to where they're hidden. The devils squeal quickly enough if it hurts – I've seen it often. And get Kimbelinus. I can't believe you let him get away."

"He is a brave man. Have you fought him?"

"No, of course – no—"

"He is a great swordsman. They are not all dolts, sir, these barbarians. Dirty and undisciplined, perhaps, but fighters to a man."

"Bloody murderers! This place needs to be rid of them! Now you have possession of the fort, get the place cleaned up! My men will get the mines working again and recruit the natives who want work. And those who don't, come to that. They are a lazy bunch of swine, but a good crack of the whip gets them moving."

Theo did not reply. Minna could see by the stiffening of his body that he was having a hard time keeping his temper. He pushed his chair back and stood up.

"I will take my leave, sir."

"Very well. But talk to my head of mines before you go, and agree with him on a plan of action."

The head of mines was a native-born man named Pir who, as a mining expert, had thrown in his lot with the Roman masters merely to get paid for doing a job. He quite quickly admitted that Julius was a swine, but shrugged his shoulders and said, "He pays me well. I have my home here, my wife and family. What Kimbelinus might think of me is of no matter.

The mines mean wealth. Where there is money, there is always squabbling. It's the same the world over."

He laughed. "If Kimbelinus is out of the way, we can go back to work. But we don't want to be caught unawares. You must make the country safe. We don't want to have our throats cut for our trouble."

"No. We'll do our job and you do yours. Come down to the fort at Navio and we can make plans. If you wish, I will send you an escort."

"No, there's men here who can accompany me if necessary. Perhaps tomorrow? I can show you the mines."

"Very well. I will expect you."

"At least that's someone I can work with," Theo said to Minna as they left the villa on their horses. "But that Julius is a swine. If he thinks I take orders from him, he's mistaken."

Theo wasn't good at taking orders, Minna knew.

"Come, we've done our work for the day," he said. "Let's take the high road home. I need a good gallop to blow that dolt out of my mind. Let's go to the top of the mountain and see how the land lies."

With which, he switched Caractacus from the beaten road and turned him onto the slope of the great hill that bounded the valley. Minna swung Silva after him and the two horses, finding the springy turf under their feet, broke into a gallop and set their faces to the bright horizon that swung above.

VIII

It was the first but not the last gallop Minna had with Theo over the great flanks of the hills to the north. Theo, now his own commander, exercised his horse Caractacus in his leisure time and if Minna chose to exercise Silva at the same time no one cared to remark upon it.

The winter days were drawing out and at times a warm sun chose to make an appearance; the camp was fully established, relations with the vicus outside the crumbled walls were now friendly and Theo's men were content for a while with the daily routine. Soon another battle would come, but they were prepared. For the time being they were glad of the rest.

The camp followers' quarters were on the riverside edge of the fort. Their possessions were technically inside what remained of the walls, but the women gradually spread outside onto the cropped grass of the gentle hillside as the spring sun began to warm them. It was easy to slip down to the river to bathe and do their washing from their motley little shacks. Stuf had made Minna a splendid shelter against the outside of a bit of wall, with a well-thatched roof and sides made with woven hazel boughs. Hung inside with skins and with a thick bed of straw and bracken to lie on at night, with Fortis beside her, it was as good as any villa to Minna's mind. It was her own place. The women had tended to separate into their own private areas, some using the wagons, some the tents: their quarters had grown like a vicus on the edge of the fort. It was a natural village. Occa had an old tent near to Minna's shack.

"If only we could stay settled here!" she said once to Minna.

But her man Gaius had five more years to do in the army and she could do nothing else but follow him.

She belonged to the army as did he, and depended on it for her food and living.

Minna too was fond of this base as winter gave way to spring and they established a routine of domestic life. But lying over them all was the knowledge that it was sooner or later going to end in violence. Theo wasn't very good at waiting for things to happen. He kept sending out scouts to look for signs of the enemy, and he ordered Draco to go spying on Caractacus, who could travel much farther than the foot soldiers.

Minna said to him, "How do you know Draco will come back, now you've given him back his horse?"

"I trust him."

"He told me Kimbelinus is his father's cousin. Did you know that? I don't know how he can fight against his own kin."

This news startled Theo.

"By the gods, if he takes Caractacus to join the enemy I shall hunt him down like a wild boar. I suffered enough in winning Caractacus – I'll not lose him now!"

But Draco came back. He reported a force of wild-looking men camping in a valley some two days' march to the east, apparently collecting under Kimbelinus's orders. But of Kimbelinus himself there was no sign. He was apparently roving the hills farther on, collecting as many men as he could, until he considered he had enough to well outnumber the Romans.

Theo was pleased with the news. He congratulated Draco but – Minna noticed – did not let him take Caractacus out again. He sent Stuf, the perfect spy, to keep an eye on what was happening. Stuf lived off the country like the native he was; he blended in, moved unseen, could pass as a shepherd or local idiot, whatever he chose, and was never suspected.

Theo said to Minna, "Any man who has been in the army is stamped by it – even Draco, after so short a time. A man as cunning as Kimbelinus will smell it out. But Stuf – he is his own man. Even if he meets him face-to-face, Kimbelinus will not connect him with the Roman army."

But Theo knew that Kimbelinus would have his own spies in the vicus close to the fort, and any move the army might make would be reported to the enemy. They were anxious, tense days, dragging into summer. But, with summer, the days were so lovely, the valleys steaming softly as the mist lifted in the mornings, the mountain ridge sharp and beckoning against an azure sky – it was hard to remind oneself why they were there.

"I wish it could be like this forever!" Minna sighed to Occa one morning as they sat together brewing their breakfast gruel over the communal fire.

Occa grunted assent. Then she said that Kimbelinus killed all women and children in his path. "What will become of us?"

"No. Our army will keep them back!" Minna cried. "You know they will! And besides, Theo has said – he told me – that we will be hidden in the woods when the time comes. We won't stay here in the fort. Of course we will be safe. You mustn't worry."

Minna had already looked out for a possible site where they could hide. Stuf had found the perfect place across the river, sheltered by a small crag of rocks behind, yet hidden too from the river by a thick band of scrub.

"I know the place to go. I will take you there."

"And if my man is killed, what then?" Occa, having started on her woes, was going to voice them all. "I would go back to Camulodunum, but how, with no one to guide me? And if he is not killed, we go on marching north. They say the country is wild and terrible and the barbarians from Caledonia always attacking – what sort of life is that for a woman?"

Minna didn't think it sounded too good either, but she wasn't given to lingering on future possibilities.

"Occa, the commander guards his women well. Don't be afraid. Maybe he will leave a force here, to join the legion who will come to take over the fort when he goes on. Who knows? Gaius is nearly old enough to retire. Surely too old to start a new fighting life on the wall."

"Gaius will not leave the commander. Gaius is a stupid soldier, faithful to death. He is my man, but the army comes first. He will follow Theodosius until his last breath."

And so will I, Minna thought.

But meanwhile, Theo, with heavy responsibilities to bear, liked to take an hour or two of leisure when he could by riding out on Caractacus to make himself more familiar with the land he guessed he would soon be fighting over. Kimbelinus had escaped before because of his intimate knowledge of the country. Theo was not going to let that happen again. By riding out along the ridge of the high hill above the main valley he had a view of the country as far as the eye could see for miles in every direction. After his first visit there alone he could not resist telling Minna to accompany him on Silva. Not a man himself for being stunned by the beauties of nature, he could not help this time wanting to share the beauty of it with Minna. Just as she had always loved the sea and its myriad permutations in different lights, so he knew that she could not fail to be entranced by the view.

The sight of the land going away in every direction under the canopy of a sky still pearly in the east and flaming red in the west was breathtaking. Ridge after ridge marched into hazy distance to north and west; to the east it fell away into forest, bright in its summer garb, alive with birdsong. Buzzards and a single pair of eagles wheeled into infinity. Theo pulled Caractacus to a halt on the highest point of the ridge and smiled as Minna looked incredulously around her. She had never seen infinities like this in Essex.

"And look, there once was a fort built right here," Theo said. "There were native people here long before we Romans ever came. You can see the outline of their defenses. It must be the most exposed fort in the land – think of the cold winds up here!"

Minna, who thought of herself as a Roman, having

lived beside the army all her life, said, "No wonder they hate us, taking their territory."

"It's nothing new, Minna. Conquer or be conquered. It's the history of the world. It will never change."

As they rode along the crest, reveling in the golden light of the sinking sun, watching their shadows lengthening ahead of them, Minna thought of Occa's anxieties, the coming bloodshed, the march to the North (should they survive)…none of it made sense on an evening like this. Yet she could not say this to Theo. She was filled with wonder at the beauty all around her and could not relate it to what lay ahead.

"We'll go down here," Theo said. "It's steep. Be careful."

But Minna knew Silva was as sure-footed as a goat. A sheep track led steadily down. There were indentations in the smooth slope where streams came down and the horses had to scramble across them. In one of these fissures Theo pulled up suddenly and slipped down from Caractacus to examine the ground.

"Footprints," he said to Minna. "A strange place to find them."

A steep wall of crags faced them, with the stream tumbling down at the foot of the rocks. Their way lay quite easily around the end of the crag. But looking into the shadows where the stream sprung from, Minna could see a dark slit in the rock, the entrance to a cave.

"People come here," Theo said. "I wonder why?"

"Is it a mine?"

"If it was worked there would be a bigger entrance, more trodden. I don't think it's a mine. But it's used. Maybe it's the hiding place for Julius's ingots."

Julius was forever goading Theo to find his lost treasure. He insisted that it could not have been taken far, as his men would have spotted any serious movement of animals carrying heavy gear. Theo had sent his men on a few desultory searches but considered it not to be the army's job. When Kimbelinus was routed, Julius could come looking himself.

"I think we should take a look," Theo said.

"It's nearly dark. It's horrible here," said Minna.

"You can stay with the horses. I'm going to look."

"You have no light!"

"Ah, but I have. My faithful Benoc never lets me travel without the necessities of life. I've torches and flints and tinder – the very best. Benoc is forever looking for a better flint than the one we've already got."

Minna had noticed that Caractacus's saddlecloth

always had bulging pockets in it and two oil-soaked torches of pine were strapped on either side.

"They say there are some very large caves around here – or so I've heard in the vicus. But I've never had time to go exploring. Ask Stuf. He knows about them. There might be a big one here. All the entrances are tiny slits, or just holes in the ground. Come on, Minna, this could be exciting."

Theo was back to being a boy again, playing with fire just as they had done as children. Once he had set fire to his tunic and burned his backside before Cerdic beat it out. It made Minna laugh to think about it.

"I'll come with you!"

While Theo started making fire, Minna tied up the horses' bridles and hobbled them with some hobbling cords that she always carried. Looking into the fissure in the rocks she did not find the prospect very inviting, but if Theo wanted her to accompany him how could she refuse?

After about ten minutes Theo got the vital spark that ignited the tinder. He set the tinder to one of the oiled torches and waited, swearing, while it writhed and smoked without flame. Minna got some more tinder, seeing the need, and, after some critical blowing and more swearing, the torch suddenly burst into flame.

"Thank the gods! Take the spare torch, Minna. They won't give us much time, but perhaps enough."

He scrambled up the rocks to the mouth of the cave and disappeared inside. The torch showed, once through the narrow slit, a passage just high enough to walk upright and wide enough to take two people. It curved away into the mountain between black, dripping walls. The way underfoot was very muddy, made into slime by the constant drips of icy water from the roof.

"But look," Theo said, "it's well used! It's full of prints. Either it leads to a silver mine, or the storehouse we're looking for."

He hurried on and Minna, hating the dank feel of the icy mine, struggled to keep up with him. It was hard to keep a footing on the slimy floor and she fell once or twice, but Theo was not looking back. She began to wish she had stayed outside to watch the horses. In one place the roof came very low and they had to bend uncomfortably to get by. The walls closed in and the torch smoked and flickered. Without the light, Minna thought she would scream. The farther they went in, the more she hated it. It was like being inside a tomb, cold as death. But Theo did not think of turning back. Minna knew when the torch burned out and he lit the second he would be forced to turn back but until then there was no respite.

But suddenly the cramped roof, scraping the backs of their crouched shoulders, gave way. The torch flared up and they emerged from the horrible little hole into a large cavern. Theo held the torch up high but the light was not strong enough to show the whole extent of the cave, so large was it. So strange! The sound of dripping water echoed, magnified, around the walls; the air was cold as ice. Minna found she was shivering, or trembling, she did not know which. Her whole body shook. They were under the mountain, under the earth, like being dead.

"Just look at it! What a hiding place!" Theo was enthusing. "Give me the other torch – I want to see how far it goes."

Minna handed it over and Theo lit it from the one in his hand. With both torches going they could see to the far side of the cave, and other exits, cracks and tunnels scooped out of the walls, coming in – or going out. The one they had entered by was one of the most insignificant. In the middle of the cave was a pile of stuff covered with a rough blanket.

"The ingots?"

Theo stepped forward, but as he did so they both heard the echo of a voice. Far away, it seemed to ricochet around the roof, more a whisper than a shout. It was impossible to know where it came from. Theo stopped in his tracks and lowered the torches.

"Stay still!"

They froze, listening. Soft voices, as if in conversation, echoed strangely around the large cave. A laugh and then a shout, and then silence.

"By the gods, if we're caught in here!"

Theo was out of uniform, unarmed, just a cloak over his shoulders. He lowered the torches and turned to Minna.

"I shall have to put these out. We don't want to be seen," he whispered. "We'll back up against the wall, stay hidden. I daresay their lights will be poor. We must hope for the best."

"Oh Theo, no!"

The darkness terrified Minna. But Theo dropped the old torch on the floor and stamped on it, kicked it away, then grasped Minna by the wrist. He pulled her over to the nearest wall of the cave, then dropped the second torch and stamped it out. The blackness came down like a curtain, like doom, so dark that if one's eyes were open or shut it was just the same.

"Don't let go of me," he whispered.

The voices were coming nearer. They seemed to be coming from the same tunnel Theo and Minna had come in by. Minna thought suddenly of the horses left by the entrance and felt a sob rise in her throat. She tried hard to keep a hold on her panic. But Theo pulled her close against him, and shrugged the thick cloak up over their heads. The darkness in Theo's embrace was kinder than the darkness outside, but as black, as hideous. Minna tried to stop her trembling. Theo held her close and she felt the warmth of his body on her shakes, his voice in her ear.

"Don't be frightened! We shall be all right."

But he had no sword on him, no light, nothing. How many men were there? If they were seen it would be all over for them.

All was silence, save for the dripping water, and once or twice from far away an oath, a kicked stone clattering. Minna began to wonder if they had gone another way, or turned back. Theo eased the cloak from over their heads.

"Where are they?"

Then, suddenly, quite close, a laugh and a shouting conversation. A glimmer of light showed from the tunnel. Theo pulled the cloak back. He could feel Minna shaking and held her close for comfort. What a scrape to have gotten into, against all his training! He was aghast at his stupidity. He, the commander of a cohort, to have gone out unarmed and play at exploring caves…thank the gods he had no higher command to report to. They had trusted him to work alone! He had an army to shortly lead into battle, and here he was caught playing silly games, like a little child.

Minna had no way of knowing how Theo's thoughts ran. He did not seem frightened, as she was frightened, but strong and brave. She clung to him.

The men came into the cave. Theo and Minna could not see them, only guess at the number – four or five? – smell the pungent stink of a torch, listen to the rough native voices in dialect so thick even Minna could not understand them. They seemed to stand around; there was the sound of something heavy being dragged across the rock floor. Were they looking for anybody, having seen the horses outside? It did not appear so. Perhaps the horses had moved away out of sight; even hobbled they could travel quite far, jumping the two front hobbled legs together. Both Caractacus and Silva were adept at moving this way. If the men were ignorant of their presence, what luck!

They only had to explore the walls with their torch and they would have found them.

But the short life of the torch hurried them on. Their voices receded quite quickly and in a few moments the glimmer of light had disappeared and only the strange echo of distant voices reverberated around the roof of the cavern, like whispering. Theo lowered the cloak to look around but now the dark was absolute.

They were alone, with just the eternal loud dripping noise and the dark. The dark!

Minna put her face in Theo's chest and sobbed.

"They went out a different way," Theo murmured. "They went out the other side of the cave. There must be a way straight through."

He stroked her hair in an absent-minded way.

"Come on, Minna. We've been lucky, can't you see? We'll go back the way we came."

"How do we find it?"

"We follow this left-hand wall. There is no exit on this side save the one we came in on."

"Can't we find the torch and light it again?"

"No. I used all the tinder. Here, take my hand. Don't let go."

His voice was calm and reassuring. Was he not frightened at all? Minna wondered. She was ashamed of herself, but could not help it. Her whole body would not stop trembling. But his hand was hard and warm.

Never had dark been so dark! Theo held her by his right hand and with his left followed the rock wall. The icy water ran over their feet. They had no idea if or when they left the cave. Minna could not convince herself that they would find the right way. Perhaps they were following a blind crack into a dead end? She had terrible visions of being unable to find the way out, of being immured like a witch buried alive, of never seeing the light again, of dying. To be alone with Theo – her dearest wish – but under such awful circumstances…!

Suddenly Theo swore, hitting his head against rock. Minna nearly screamed.

"What is it?"

"It's a good sign – we must be where the roof comes down low. Do you remember, we had to stoop? We must be on the right track."

It was true. The roof made them bend double. Still

Theo's hand held tightly to Minna's. They edged along, feeling the wall.

"If it's right, we should see light soon," Minna said, hopefully.

"I think it might be dark outside by now."

More dark, but with the blessed light of moon and stars! What bliss that would be! Perhaps a glow of the late sun in the west…never had the earth seemed so beautiful in her mind, with the smell of sweet grass and mist, not this dreadful icy dankness binding them around.

Slipping and slithering, grazed and cut by sharp corners of rock, shivering with cold, at last a vestige of slightly less dark filtered into sight. Sight! Minna had thought she would never see again.

"There," Theo said, and stopped. He sounded as relieved as Minna felt, but there was doubt in his voice.

"If they saw the horses, they might be waiting for us. Or, more likely, they've taken them."

"Oh no!"

"Sssh. If they're there, they will hear us."

He stayed pressed against the wall, listening. But all was silent outside. He waited. He pulled Minna towards him and put his arm around her.

"Poor little Minna," he whispered. "What frights I give you! How stupid I was just now. We mustn't tell anyone of this. I shall send a guard to see if this is the ingot store. I will say we saw a crack in the cliff, and footprints. Don't tell anyone how stupid I was, Minna, not even Stuf. It will do me no good. If a man of mine had been so stupid, I'd have put him on hard labor for a year."

"Oh Theo, you're not stupid! I won't tell Stuf, or anybody, I promise."

"I wish you could join the army, Minna. I'd have you a centurion in no time."

Minna giggled. "I would kill Kimbelinus for you!"

"Ah, no, that's my job. Soon. He has mustered his men, over a thousand my scouts tell me. At last we might see some action."

A thousand! Their cohort numbered half that, yet Theo sounded confident.

"This adventure is nothing, Minna, compared with what lies ahead. Perhaps you should have stayed curling Julia's hair for her. It would have been safer."

"No. I wouldn't change it, never."

"Come then. There's no one out there. Let's see if our horses are still there."

Still holding her hand, he started on again towards the blessed exit from the mountain. The evening light was like daylight compared with what they were emerging from, and the fresh smell of the mountain grass blew in like nectar. They stumbled out of the hole, soaked and shivering. Theo unfastened his cloak and wrapped it around Minna as they stood looking down the valley from the mouth of the crevice. There was no sign of the horses.

"At least we're alive. We're free. We must thank the gods for our deliverance. But I would like Caractacus back."

"And Silva!"

After all that had happened, Minna couldn't believe she might have lost Silva.

Theo was looking for hoof prints.

"They might have made for home," Minna said.

The horses were fed in the evening and had new comfortable stables where the feed would be waiting. As they came out of the fissure onto the side of the hill Minna could see the lights of the fort flickering below, along the valley.

"They can't have gotten very far, hobbled. Here, in the mud, look." Theo was scouring the ground.

"This way. You're right, heading for home."

And as they skidded and scrambled down the steep ground they caught sight of the two horses grazing below, Silva's light coat showing up in the dusk. Minna gave a shout of joy. Silva's head came up and he gave an answering whinny. He half turned, hopping a few paces towards her. Caractacus put his head up, but did not follow.

"There, how he loves you, Minna! My horse doesn't care for me a bit."

Theo came bounding down after her, his doubts cast aside. Caractacus waited for him. They unbound the horses and rode on down the valley. Minna's thoughts were brimming now with love and joy and astonishment at what happened.

"Don't tell!" Theo reminded her as they rode into camp.

She laughed. If only she could be back again in the darkness under Theo's cloak, with his arms around her! If she had not been so frightened, how she would have savored those moments! But now it was too late.

IX

"Draco's deserted," Stuf said.

Minna gasped. "Deserted!"

"He came to me last night and told me he was going. Asked me to get him some clothes. He's going to join Kimbelinus. He can't stand being told what to do all the time, the drill, the training. He's taken his sword, left his uniform, gone."

"Does Theo know?"

"Yes. Titus discovered it at roll-call and told him."

"He's out of his mind, going back to join that rabble! And if he's taken when the battle comes he'll be executed. Didn't he think of all that?"

"Yes. I think he did. But he's gone back to the life he's always known. It came hard for him, being a soldier – the discipline, after roaming around the countryside all the time with his crazy father. He only became a soldier because he had no choice. Theo killed his father and put Draco in prison. As if you don't remember!"

"I remember it only too well! But the army's been good for Draco, you know that. And Theo trusted him! Draco told me he would follow Theo anywhere."

"I suppose this lying around, waiting, gave him time to think about it, get bored. It's over now, anyway, the waiting. A few days…they're collecting up the valley. It's time you moved out. Out of the way."

It was a hot, perfect, summer morning. Minna had gone to the cookhouse to get a bone for Fortis and had been playing with him on the grass slope that led down to the river. Most of the women were doing chores around their campsite.

"Where are we to go then?" she queried. "That place across the river you found?"

"I'll get you settled there. I think Theo is coming down to give you orders. He's in a terrible temper, I warn you. About Draco."

Theo had had such hopes of Draco, Minna knew, and had given him preference and the promise of his joining his bodyguard. He admired the boy's spirit, his stubborn courage and the swordsmanship he had learned from his father. How crazy of Draco to have thrown such prospects away! Yet Minna could see how little he had in common with the hardbitten soldiers in Theo's command and how difficult it was for him, after a life of total freedom, to buckle down to the tough discipline of the soldier's life. He was a free spirit born and bred. Cerdic had hated it too, in spite of a far more disciplined upbringing.

Minna, on edge like all of them waiting for the battle, now found it hard to take in the news of Draco's defection. But she could see how it must have been for him. She was disappointed, having always thought that Draco would one day be her friend, in spite of his having given her little encouragement. But not now.

Stuf nudged her suddenly and scrambled to his feet. Theo was coming down the slope towards them. Minna jumped up. This was not the Theo of the black tunnel, holding her close, laughing at their adventure, but the commander of the Roman army in full army uniform, his black eyes burning with fury underneath the plume of his helmet.

"Did Draco speak to you?" he snapped at Minna.

"No. No, I never saw him!"

"He'll be sorry, that's all I can say, when we've wiped out those swine and the river runs with their blood and he's part of it. Put up your things here, you've got to go. It will be no place for women this time tomorrow. I want you out of the way."

Was this to be her parting from him? Minna thought, choked, as she started to gather up her sleeping things. If he were to be killed, would this be the face she would remember, hostile and angry? She wanted to ask him about the horses, but she did not dare open her mouth.

"I'll send a man down to you later, with provisions to see you through. Keep hidden, the forest is close enough. I expect you to be gone within the hour."

He did not even glance at her, turning on his heel and stalking back towards his headquarters. Stuf looked at Minna and shrugged.

"I'll help you down there. That's a good place we found. You can always back out up the valley if you have to."

"Call on that toad Julius!" Minna exclaimed.

"No, he's run off. Scared for his skin. Didn't even wait for his precious ingots!"

"Theo's keeping them," Minna said. The cave they had discovered had indeed been the hiding place of the precious ingots. The army had moved them down to the fort, where they lay in a deep chamber in what had once been the fort's guardroom.

"He said if Julius wants them he can come and collect them."

Cast down by Theo's bad temper, Minna was thankful for Stuf's help. There was nobody who knew more than Stuf about making a comfortable camp in rough conditions. When he had finished, it was so cleverly made that some of the women couldn't even find the site. They were complaining bitterly about their lot – not surprisingly, Minna thought. For herself, she could think of nothing but the coming battle and the danger to Theo, the danger to them all. Her grief for poor Cerdic kept returning and in the afternoon she went with Fortis to the site where his ashes had been scattered to the four winds and kneeled there for some time praying – in her fashion – to whatever gods came to mind, to keep Cerdic happy in the afterworld, to keep Theo safe, to give them victory when the battle came. It all seemed now such a far cry from her family life down in the south. How she had longed for excitement then!

The late afternoon sun slanted down through the trees, no wind stirred, and far, far away down the valley she could hear the disturbance of the rabble army collecting under Kimbelinus. Near at hand she could hear the sound of the river running over its stony bed and the flapping of ducks' wings as they washed and played in the deep pool under the trees; she could hear the sweet birdsong above her head and the distant lowing of cattle as they were driven away from the vicus to safety on the hillsides. A perfect summer evening…it was hard to believe what was going to happen when the next dawn broke. Perhaps Cerdic was well out of it. On the burned earth lay some wild flowers some of the women had laid there. Fortis whined as he always did when he sensed he was near his old master and came to Minna as she knelt, to lick her hands and find consolation. Minna buried her face in his yellow hair.

"Oh, Fortis, if only it were over and we were all safe!"

But it would never be over if Theo had his way; there would always be a battle ahead. She would never have peace if she followed Theo. She would get old and haggard with worry before her time like poor Occa.

Impatiently she jumped to her feet. She must think on more practical things; the most important was how to make Silva safe from the battle. Surely Theo would not want him in the battle, even if he wanted Caractacus to hand? Stuf must find out. She went back along the riverside to find him.

Stuf already knew about the horses.

"Theo wants Caractacus up in the fort but not Silva. He doesn't want Silva."

"Oh, the gods be praised! Can I get him now?"

"No. He said the men would bring him down at dusk."

So there was nothing to do now but wait. The sun slipped behind the hills that blocked in the western end of the valley and a soft, damp haze slipped across the river. Minna sat beside the fire as Stuf fed it with cut branches, making it ready to cook the evening meal. She realized she took for granted his skills at making life comfortable; she took for granted his ready humor, his easy composure at whatever life threw at him, his kindness to her. She took him completely for granted. She knew then that, if he were not there, her life would be very lonely. It was strange how, with the threat of the impending horrors now so close, she was suddenly evaluating her life, seeing it as if it were from another's eyes. How much she owed to Stuf, from the moment she had more or less fallen into his arms at the start of the journey…

"You're not going to join battle tomorrow, are you?" she asked him sharply.

"No! You know me. I can't kill anything unless it's to eat. I'm staying out of the way."

"We depend on you so much," she said.

"Oh, come! You're the last one to depend on anybody! Just make sure you've got your dagger on you tomorrow, that's all."

"I've always got it on me. The one you gave me."

"That's fine then. Just in case."

Soon some men came down with the oxen and donkeys, driving them along the edge of the river, past their camp and out along the valley. One man came last with Silva.

Minna put him on a long tether nearby, where the

grazing was good, but he had been fed and was not hungry. He stood dozing. His summer coat gleamed in the dusk. He was so beautiful! If only all was peace, Minna thought, she could buy one of the native hill-ponies and breed horses with Silva as her stud horse… what a sweet life that would be! She drank in the peace…never, it seemed, had a summer evening been more beguiling.

She cleared up the supper things and took the wooden platters down to the river to scrape clean with sand and pebbles. It was dark now and the night was silent. Not a sound came from the fort. It was a time of waiting.

Waiting for the battle.

X

It did not take Draco long to realize he might have done the wrong thing. In the cold dawn light, before the sun came over the hilltops, he was kicked awake and ordered to get into line. This was not the same as the evening before, when he had made himself known to Kimbelinus and had been welcomed with a stinking embrace and a roar of welcome. Now he was as lowly a soldier as he had been with his Roman companions – worse, he could sense at once that this army was totally wild, undisciplined and completely inexperienced in battle. Only their mad enthusiasm sustained them, kindled by the despotic Kimbelinus. They were armed with as motley a collection of weapons as Draco had ever seen: swords, meat cleavers, clubs, javelins, homemade spears, even shovels and pitchforks. Thank the gods he had brought his own Roman gladius! But the closer he came to the fight, the less he felt any ambition to use it. What was wrong with him? He had killed in the past, as a boy with his marauding father; he was impeccably trained in killing by Theo; he knew he could hold his own against any but the very best in a sword-fight...but where was the motivation now? He had no desire at all to kill his past companions in the Roman army; he had no desire to kill his own rough kind, these men he had defected to; he just wanted to run away into the hills and hide. To be a deserter twice over. What sort of a man did that make him?

As the rabble of men started to move forward down the valley, chattering and excited (not in any semblance of marching order), he thought of his Roman companions; they were no doubt by now well fed and well prepared, ready to line up under their well-rehearsed formation of shields, protected by good armor, confident in the strategy of their leader, not talking much but eager all the same to get this battle out of the way so that they could continue their march north…why had he thought deserting from them was such a good idea? He had acted on an impulse. He had had a dream of his father, in which his father had poured scorn on him for becoming a Roman soldier. But what choice had he had, imprisoned, when the only release possible was to join the army? There had been no choice. In his dream he had tried to tell his father this, but his father had hit him over the head with an iron rod. Draco had woken up at this and found that the man sleeping beside him had flung out an arm in turning over and hit him in the face. Waking from the dream had been a welcome release from the wrath of his father, so well-remembered. He shuddered. All his father had taught him was sword-fighting. He knew nothing of order, learning, friendship, love – all the things the people around him took for granted. The stupid girl Minna knew more than he did about living. Stumbling over the rough terrain in the midst of Kimbelinus's army (could it be called an army at all? he wondered) he was speared by a totally unaccustomed flood of self-pity; cold, hungry, friendless, probably about to be killed or injured by a well-fed, well-trained, unafraid Roman soldier, what use was he on this earth? His spirits were at rock-bottom.

The sun was just spearing down the valley, teetering on the high hill to the east. The forest was loud with birdsong. The people from the vicus had retired with their animals to the hillsides to keep out of the way (did they care who won? Probably not, as long as they could live in peace) and the valley echoed to the lowing and bleating and crowing of moving animals and fowl. The Roman trumpet sounded again, and now Draco could see the cohort standard raised to the breeze. The soldiers were silhouetted along the crest of the fort's highest ground, and Draco knew that the commander was waiting to kill Kimbelinus, and his army was waiting to kill them all and he, Draco, was on the wrong side. And that he, Draco, had made a very bad mistake.

How could Draco know that the commander, standing on his high ground watching the wild advance of the barbarian army, was as terrified as Draco himself? But such was Theo's training he did not betray it by one flicker of an eyelid. He had been preparing to do this job all his life, but for all his training he was inexperienced in real battle. He had only been given his command because his superiors wanted to get rid of him – let the young firebrand go north and get killed, had been the gossip. He was perfectly aware of it. And now here he was, doing what he wanted to do, facing an enemy that outnumbered him two to one, without any prospect of reinforcement. Fear was laced with an almost unbearable excitement. The howls of the enemy, like the howls of wolves, rose like strange music to the accompaniment of his own trumpeter, who stood at his elbow.

"Pila prepare," he snapped to the trumpeter, who was a boy of Draco's age. The trumpet signal flew out clear and unwavering, and the line of expert javelin-throwers in the front line lifted their weapons. Theo caught the eye of the centurion in charge and saw his hesitation, waited for his nod. The man could estimate distance to an inch. The man nodded, Theo gave a sharp command to the trumpeter and as its urgent note shrilled out, the great, heart-stopping whir of the cloud of released spears sang over their heads, the whistle of death. The enemy scarcely had a shield between them, and the attack that would have been stopped by a

Roman shield made a deadly impact on the advancing enemy. The front line stumbled and fell in heaps, the howls of wrath turned to unearthly screams. Theo gave the signal again for the second flight. The trumpet rang out and the javelins whistled again. Theo felt his blood pounding with joy at the lethal effect of these simple weapons: another rank of screaming fallers and a slight hesitation in the mob behind. But a stentorian voice roared encouragement and Theo was able to pick out Kimbelinus. Like himself, he was closely guarded and in a position keeping to a ridge of higher ground, so that he was able to get a view of the situation. He was shouting now and jabbing his finger in the direction of the lowest point of the fort. His men, still running down the hill towards the road below, wheeled to his directions. Theo shouted to his front line to regroup to face them, and then sent a messenger to the far side of his line to tell them to stop any encircling movement at all costs. It was shortly to be hand-to-hand fighting and then neither he nor Kimbelinus would have much chance to organize their armies.

But he was desperate not to lose sight of Kimbelinus. That was his man, to take for his own.

By all the gods, the moment had arrived! Theo saw

the roaring barbarians fall on his own men's shields and by sheer weight of numbers they caused the line to buckle in several places. Theo leaped down with his bodyguard to reinforce them, his voice giving them heart. Where the line fell, his men were into the gap like lightning, swords flashing, until the shields rose again and the line moved forward, inspired by those who had come so quickly to their aid. Theo shouted encouragement; his men regrouped and surrounded him.

"We'll go for Kimbelinus. Keep by me! Where's Titus?"

He gave his second-in-command instructions to keep the fort from being infiltrated from the sides; his own lack of numbers made this the most serious threat and one he would like to oversee himself, but he trusted Titus. And either killing or capturing Kimbelinus would put this whole rabble to rout, he was sure, for they had no discipline beyond the man's goading. If he himself were to be killed, his army had a well-rehearsed drill to carry on without him; there would be no faltering. But he doubted that Kimbelinus had made any such precautionary plans.

Kimbelinus had now come forward with his men and

was hacking away at the center of Theo's front line. Theo saw his chance and sent a messenger quickly forward: "Fall aside and let him through and close up behind him." It was a dangerous move, he recognized that. His bodyguard closed up to stem the tide through the gap and see it closed again, and Theo, drawing his sword, got his first good view of Kimbelinus. He was in full armor, unlike most of his army, and he was attended by a dozen or so swordsmen whose expertise was apparent. In the gap two good Romans fell before the two bodyguards clashed. Kimbelinus charged and Theo met him face-to-face, unable any longer to give orders, only praying that the tide of men following their leader would be stemmed. What a rabble! Most of them had no swords, only knives and clubs and the dreadful ax; they were easy prey for his trained soldiers. Not so the man himself, and his near supporters. Theo already knew Kimbelinus was an expert swordsman, but he was confident too of his own skill. As he engaged with him he felt a surge of tingling euphoria – to be up against a man of such caliber! It was so long since he had engaged with such a worthy fighter – not since Cintus – and the sparks flying from his blade, the glorious clash of steel, was such a spur to his senses that he shouted out loud in a surge of violent excitement, as crazy as the roaring Kimbelinus himself. There was no thoughtful parrying, but head-on viciousness – he to Kimbelinus and his men to the fierce group that was giving him protection.

Fighting Kimbelinus was of a different order to Theo's practice. There was no brain used, no feinting, no real expertise, just brute strength wielding fearsome slashes and thrusts at close quarters. In close contact Kimbelinus used the weight of his huge body to try to get Theo on the ground and Theo had no alternative but to back smartly away. But then his sword would flash and catch his lumbersome opponent before the man could level his own sword. Blood flowed from the barbarian's upper arm and thigh. He bellowed like an ox at slaughter and one of his men flung around with his terrible two-bladed ax and threw himself at Theo. Theo's sword flew upwards and the ax with the hand and half the arm still attached went spinning over his head. The blood spurted into Theo's face, half-blinding him. He jumped back as Kimbelinus came at him again, but one of his men, throwing off his own adversary, stopped Kimbelinus with a swift jab in the side and Theo was able to engage again, with such swift ferocity that this time Kimbelinus had to fall back.

Blood was flowing from cuts in his upper body, and Theo was aware that he too was not unscathed, but the fighting spirit quenched both doubt and pain. Their swords clashed, throwing sparks, and they closed again, gasping and swearing.

But Theo's bodyguard was steadily decimating Kimbelinus's men. Theo was unaware how the rest of the battle was going but realized that Kimbelinus's support was faltering and one or two of his own men, no longer engaged, hovered to protect him should he lose ground to his adversary.

One of them shouted to Theo, "They're on the run, sir!" and the other in broad Celtic shouted to Kimbelinus, "Put up your sword! Your army is beat!"

But Kimbelinus made no move to back down. The news only galvanized him to fight harder and Theo guessed he was not a man to surrender. There was little Theo's men could do when the two fighters were so closely engaged and moving so fast. Theo was desperate to disarm Kimbelinus rather than kill him; he wanted to parade him before his skeptical superiors. They would not be convinced by hearing of a killing, not without proof. But disarming the man was no easier than killing him. So equally matched, one by sheer weight and anguish, the other by skill and intelligence, they struggled to conclude the fight.

Then, for a moment, exhausted, they both backed off to get breath. And in that sudden stillness between them they became aware of the terrible screams of the dying below them and the triumphant roars of the Roman army. The noise, crowned by the trumpet's crowing, fell on their ears as if from another planet, glorious for Theo, terrible for Kimbelinus. They both instinctively downed their swords, and Theo's men moved in instantly and challenged Kimbelinus to give up his weapon. He spat at them and swore.

At the same moment Titus appeared at Theo's side.

"It's a victory, sir! Praise be to the gods that you are safe! Give up your sword!" he shouted at Kimbelinus. "Look at your men running away! Stop them if you can!"

He was euphoric, laughing, although blood was running down his face. Theo, exhausted, felt suddenly faint with the realization of his victory; everything that he had most feared was now behind him! He had proved himself – his army had routed a force twice its size! The piles of bodies that he could now see heaped below the walls of the old fort were nearly all those of the barbarians, and the screaming and groans of the wounded were a lament that did not move him – the lament of the vanquished, music to his ears.

He turned and flung his arm around Titus and cried, "The gods are with us, Titus! Well done! Well done!"

In that moment – it happened so quickly, no one quite took in the sequence of events – Kimbelinus lifted his sword to plunge it into Theo's back. And in the sliver of a second it took him to launch it, a slender figure leaped between Theo and the sword and took the full impact of the thrust in his back. The blow toppled them both to the ground and they lay together, the jeweled hilt of Kimbelinus's sword quivering out of Draco's back.

Stuf decided to emerge when he heard the trumpet calling victory and see what victory looked like. He wasn't squeamish, after all.

The same hillside that had become home during the last weeks, where they had lain in the sun between exercises and sat drinking in the evening, now looked like a nightmare picture of some hellish afterlife, covered with dead and dying bodies. A minor skirmish, no doubt, to make small impression on the Emperor, but to unaccustomed eyes a truly dreadful sight. Few of the bodies were those of the Roman army; they were a tangled pile of blood-soaked peasants, missing arms and legs and even heads, or half-clove in two like cooked chickens. Many still groaned and cried and some of the older soldiers were dispatching the worst wounded with deep stabs to the heart. Some of the rest were attending to their own wounded, carrying them into their quarters, and the remainder were standing around trying to look as if such carnage was all in a day's work. But they trembled, Stuf noticed; their hands shook and some of the younger ones were sitting down crying. They had never been in battle before.

Stuf was shaken, in spite of not being squeamish. He felt sick and even a bit faint. He went towards Theo's tent, where the standard was still gleaming happily in the sunlight. Benoc was there, alone, setting wine beakers on the table.

"Well done for still being alive," Stuf said shakily.

"I hid in the chamber where the ingots are. Theo told me to." His voice was as shaky as Stuf's and his hands were trembling. "I will not feel it a victory until I see the commander safe," he said softly.

"If Theo is dead the men would not be cheering so," Stuf pointed out.

For there was now definitely some disturbance going on down by the corner of the old walls and the resting soldiers were getting up and starting to shout to each other. There was no alarm in their voices, but a growing excitement.

"What's happened?"

They went to the door of the tent and looked across to find out. A crowd was gathering below them, but it was being cleared peremptorily by members of Theo's bodyguard, to let through some bearers carrying a stretcher. Theo walked beside the stretcher.

"He's wounded," Benoc said sharply.

"Well, at least he's not the one on the stretcher."

It was clear that the stretcher was being given more respect than seemed natural.

The two boys frowned, curious.

Then Benoc said, "Look, Theo is holding his hand. That means. . . it can only be . . . "

"Draco," said Stuf.

Benoc was silent.

Then, as the party approached, he said, "I hope he's dead."

XI

Minna stayed in the glade where Silva was grazing while the battle raged. Silva was nervous, smelling blood, and Fortis too whined and kept his muzzle close to Minna's leg, shivering. Minna laid her head against Silva's shoulder, her cheek on his steely summer coat, so warm and sweet. The tears ran down her cheeks. How could they do this to each other? she wondered. And Theo...Theo ordering it, Theo with his sword drawn, Theo killing...was this the man she loved so much, the man who had held her close under his cloak and kept her from being so frightened, this same man who was ordering the attack, ordering the killing? She could not come to terms with it. Yet sense told her that Theo was doing what he had trained all his life to do. He wanted this above all else. She had always known it, so what was the use of pretending to be surprised?

But for her the day was a nightmare. She could not ever have imagined the horror of the noise of killing. She saw nothing, lying down beside her anxious, sweating horse, her face pressed into the sweet-smelling grass or against the quivering dog's body. As she cried, Fortis cried with weird doggy whimpers, and above his distress soared the terrible screams of men being killed over the hilltop. Sometimes trumpet blasts or shouted commands, then roars of exhilaration, or despair – how could she tell? And screams and demented shouts, shrieks, sudden lulls with a soft background of moaning and crying…it was like being in the underworld her mother used to tell her of, where bad people went to suffer after death, how she had pictured it in her childish mind. Yet never had she pictured it anything like the reality that was now assailing her. And all the time the terrible knowledge that Theo was in the thick of it, Theo was *ordering* it,

Theo *wanted* it, the Theo she loved so much. Was she crazy to love such a monster?

Yet he was kind and loving and charming and clever and funny and his men loved him just as she did, as did Benoc and Stuf and even Draco, so none of it made sense. She wept for her dreams being shattered. She wept for the horror of it. The day went on forever. How long did the battle last? She had no idea, yet she knew when it was over by the triumphant ringing out of the trumpet. The chorus of Roman cheers were suddenly louder than the chorus of groans and pitiable shrieks, and the babble of excitement that followed; surely it would not be like that if the commander had been killed. He must be safe! At that Minna was flooded with relief. She lay quivering, limp, her mind reeling. She had no idea of how much time had passed, scarcely whether it was morning or evening. But the sun still shone. The soft breeze still rustled through the treetops; a pair of ducks flew above. She rolled over and stood up. Her legs would scarcely hold her. She went and leaned on Silva, who was in a sweat of nervousness.

They were alone in the valley. Most of the other women, in spite of orders to remain, had fled away from the fighting in the direction of the Roman villa; only Occa and a couple of the older ones had stayed, and they were moaning and praying in their shelter. Minna had no wish to join them. She stayed at Silva's side, soothing him, and her soft words soothed her as well, so that she felt herself coming together, the dreadful shock wearing off. Then of course she was intensely curious to know what was going on out of her sight. She thought if she went a little way up the hill she might meet Stuf or Benoc or one of the old men who had kept out of harm's way, and from them she would learn how Theo had come through. She needn't go far enough to see the full horror of it all. But she found it hard to move, leaning against Silva's withers with her face buried in his mane.

"Thank goodness you were not in the battle!"

But after a little while Silva started to graze again, and Minna's curiosity overcame her, so she set off a little shakily on the track out of the stream and up towards the fort. Her head was still reeling. The brutality of the day was hard to accept. Yet she had known what would happen…

As she came clear of the trees she saw the familiar figure of Stuf loping down the hill towards her.

"Stuf!" she screamed, relief overwhelming her.

She ran towards him and nearly knocked him over in a frantic embrace. He held her, laughing. How could he laugh!

"Oh, Stuf! What's happened? Is Theo safe?"

"Safe enough. I came to see that you are all right. I was afraid some skirmishers might come this way. It's impossible to round up all of the enemy. Most have surrendered but some have run back up the way they came."

"Is Theo safe? Unhurt?"

Stuf stood silent for a moment, so that Minna's heart began to pulse again with fear.

"What's happened?"

Stuf shook his head. "I don't like to tell you. Yes, Theo is safe, but Draco…"

He hunkered down in front of her and told her the story. That Kimbelinus had been hacked to death by Theo's bodyguard, that Theo was blaming himself for turning his back, that Draco had given his life for Theo.

Minna gasped. "But he deserted!"

"On a stupid impulse. He must have regretted it. If he hadn't been there Theo would surely have been killed, but he took the thrust of the sword that was meant for Theo. He's still breathing but he's so gravely hurt that they hold out little hope for him."

"He's not dead!"

"I exaggerated. Good as, Minna. I'm not making this up. It was terrible. They say it happened in an instant. He just acted by instinct, like lightning."

"He loved Theo!"

"Yes, Theo inspires devotion, we all know that." Stuf's tone was dry and he smiled wryly. "Not many men are so lucky."

"I must go to Draco. I can nurse him. He mustn't die!"

"No. Don't go up there. It's a terrible scene. Theo would not want you to see it. Already the soldiers are clearing the bodies but it will take all day, Minna. Stay here. There's nothing you can do. The best surgeons are working on Draco, do not fear, before anyone. Theo has commanded them."

"He mustn't die! Oh, Stuf, he mustn't die!"

"It's in the hands of the gods, you know that. Perhaps they will smile kindly on him."

The tears ran down Minna's cheeks. Stuf put a comforting arm around her shoulders.

"Come, Minna. The battle is won, Theo is safe, it's not all bad news. Just stay here and think of all the good things and pray for Draco. There is nothing else to do. Don't come up the hill until the bodies are cleared. The sight is too dreadful. I have to go back and help but you're not to come."

Theo was safe, thank the gods – was she never satisfied? But Draco! She started sobbing again for the friendship she had tried in vain to cultivate, for the proud, brave boy she so admired and had argued so fiercely with. Yet she scarcely knew Draco, she realized, that unfathomable boy; why should she care? She wept, prayed, cuddled Fortis fiercely, the dog that knew death as she knew it. He still lay by Cerdic's pyre ashes at quiet times of the day. Minna realized with even greater despair that she wept more profoundly for Draco than she had for her own brother.

Now the sun was starting to go down and long shadows crept down from the fort. There was nothing to do but to go back to her lair. Theo would not be best pleased if she turned up now, when he was exhausted from battle and had his army to sort out. She had no place in this part of his life. She now wondered if she had any place in it at all, if this day was how it was going to be in the future. She was shaken beyond imagining.

She scrambled down to the stream-side and waded across. Silva was no longer there grazing, only the figure of old Occa, still wailing.

Minna's heart skipped a beat.

"Where's Silva?" she shouted.

"They took him! They took him! Terrible wild men, all covered in blood! We couldn't stop them!"

XII

Theo sat beside the inert body of Draco in his tent, his eyes fixed on the blood that seeped through the bindings holding together the gaping gash in the boy's body. The sword had gone right through Draco and pierced Theo's own body in the side, so that they had been spitted together in the bloody grass while Kimbelinus was hacked to bits by the Roman bodyguard.

The army surgeons had more work to do than they could cope with. Theo had waved them away from himself, which he now realized was a mistake.

He could feel the blood trickling down his side, and knew he could not stand even if he wished. He had ordered his centurions outside to command the rounding up of the prisoners, the killing of the worst wounded, the succour of their own wounded. He knew his men needed him, but he could think only of Draco, who had saved him from the biggest of the many mistakes he had made in his life. Turning his back on Kimbelinus was stupidity of the first order. The man was a savage, and Theo had treated him as if he were an honorable Roman. If he were to make many more mistakes of that order he might as well creep back to Camulodunum and be a pen-pusher again.

The battle was won; his tactics had been successful; he had lost very few men. He should be rejoicing in this simple victory. But he could not move.

"Sir?"

Benoc stood silently behind him.

"Help me, Benoc. And don't let Draco die."

He had taken Benoc for granted all his life, but never had he felt gratitude as he did now for the young man's devotion. Benoc was more skilful than even the best of the ham-fisted, brutal men that called themselves surgeons. After the expenditure of every ounce of his courage and wits to win the battle with Kimbelinus, Theo was now exhausted, yet he knew he had to stand and go out to his men who had fought like wild boars and now required his praise and leadership. All his instincts fought to stay with Draco.

"The surgeons are giving him short shrift. I know he deserted but he saved my life. I depend on you, Benoc, to save him."

"It might not be possible."

"Try."

"He could have done better. Your wound is deep."

"Kimbelinus had a fine sword. Do what you can. I can rest later."

"You should rest now. It will go on bleeding even if I sew it, unless you rest."

"So be it. Hurry up."

Benoc hurried. He did not mind hurting Theo after being reminded of Theo's devotion to the undeserving Draco, so ignored Theo's curses and groans as he stitched and swabbed the wound with burning spirit.

"You said hurry," he reminded his master, and bound the wound tightly with a ripped-up linen tunic. "Now see if you can rise. Lean on me. And pray tonight for your own deliverance. You are doing yourself no good."

He would have gotten a clout around the head for airing his opinion if Theo had had the strength, but it was all Theo could do to stand on his feet.

"Dress me. My clean...my best..."

Benoc fetched the required uniform from its chest. The leather tunic Theo had discarded was only fit now for the waste pile, but the heavy metal breastplate, although scored and dented, was serviceable. Benoc lifted it into place and did up the fastenings. Its bottom edge rested on the newly-dressed wound and Theo winced, but waved away Benoc's idea of a lump of stuffing underneath.

"It will fall out and make me look a fool. I've not far to walk."

The metaled, bejeweled belt was no more comfortable, nor the helmet on his fevered head, but Theo straightened up and took his sword, which Benoc had wiped clean, and walked out of the tent.

"See to Draco. Do not leave him!" he hissed as he went.

Benoc shrugged, biting his lip. The scene outside was terrible, but it was a victory. Would the sight of so many dead lift Theo's spirits? One assumed so. The sun was shining brightly on the scene of carnage and the cooks were already preparing a feast to reward the good soldiers for killing so many men. Theo would likely bleed to death in the night and Draco was unlikely to last that long. Benoc felt like crying, considering all these facts. He was never cut out to serve such a man as Theo. A fat tribune in his villa extorting taxes would have suited him far better. Yet he would die for Theo. Draco's willingness to do the same enraged him. And now he had to save Draco's life. If Draco died, Theo in his rage would have him flogged. If Draco didn't die...then thanks never came the way of slaves.

He turned back to the still figure lying prone on Theo's dining table. The sword had gone right through him, below his ribcage, to one side. Benoc did not know what innards were pierced, his knowledge of anatomy sketchy, but assumed nothing too vital, because the boy still lived. The wound was huge and roughly sewn together. Benoc cleaned it as he had cleaned Theo's – he stripped the filthy tunic off and washed all the mud and blood away. He felt no tenderness for this wild boy. His work over him was as ordered; he was acting like a good housemaid, tidying up. But he found a soft blanket to make a pillow for the boy's head and wrapped him warmly over the fresh bandages and tried to dribble some water into his mouth. Draco's eyes opened and he groaned, but could not speak.

"You're to live. Theo's orders," Benoc said.

Draco's eyes flickered.

He whispered, "I want…" A bubble of blood filled on his lip. Benoc wiped it away.

"What do you want?"

"Die. To…die."

And Benoc determined, in that moment, that Draco would live.

XIII

Minna screamed at Occa, "Which way did they go? How many of them? How long ago?"

The old woman was shaking and weeping, no doubt having thought the men had come to kill her. But Minna had no mercy.

"Which way?" she screamed.

Occa pointed a quavering finger up the main valley, the way the rabble army had come from.

"There. Up there."

"How long ago?"

Occa shook her head. It was a waste of time – Occa

had no numeracy and no sense of measuring time. But surely, Minna thought, she hadn't been long on the hillside with Stuf – the men couldn't have been gone more than half an hour. Her first hysteria gave way to wild conjecture. She could catch up with them! After the battle they wouldn't go far, surely? They must be worn out. Just far enough to be safe from the rounding up of prisoners.

"How many? How many were there?"

"Two. Three."

The woman couldn't even count to three!

If only Stuf had come back with her! But it was no good wasting time by going back to look for him. The men wouldn't go far, she was convinced, and the sooner she was after them the better. She daren't fetch Caractacus, in case Theo wanted him for something. She wouldn't dare take his horse, even in such an emergency, and the others were away up the valley. So there was nothing to do but snatch up her cloak and take Silva's bridle, which the men had ignored, and set off in pursuit. Not being a girl of caution, it never occurred to her to act differently. Of course, later she would realize she had acted with more haste than sense. But then, who was there to help her, save Stuf?

He would advise her not to go in the first place, so that was no good. She could not ask any of the soldiers without going to Theo first, so that was no good either. So she set off, running and stumbling along the side of the stream where Silva's hoof prints were quite clear to see. Fortis came with her, joyful again at the thought of a run, his fears forgotten. And Minna found, with the fresh urgency infusing her frame, that her shakiness too was forgotten and all her feeble fears during the day vanished. She had her precious dagger still, strapped to her leg, the one Stuf had given her when she had first left home and which she had never discarded. Anyone who hurt Silva would soon have it at his throat! How a girl of fifteen was going to get the better of three men was not a question she thought to ask, nor did she think of the danger she might be going into.

The path she followed came out onto the main road that ran down from the vicus. But the men had avoided it by turning up onto the hillside and continuing eastward along the side of the hill. It was the same way Minna had come down with Theo from their excursion in that dreadful cave. But the men were still following the direction of the main road, just riding above it so as to avoid meeting anyone. The hoof prints were quite clear setting off in that direction but later, as the ground grew firmer, they were hard to follow. But on down the valley was the obvious direction to take. The men were heading back to where they had come from, perhaps to their campsite of the night before, where there might still be food and at least a place to rest. They must be in a dreadful state after seeing so many of their comrades killed. Or were they too thick-skinned to care? Minna had no idea of what she was going into.

The day was nearly over and the bottom of the valley was growing dark. It was thickly forested, although the road was quite broad and clear. There was no longer any chance of tracking Silva; in fact little chance of finding him at all, Minna now realized, as a great weariness overcame her. But some of the broken army of Kimbelinus, the lucky ones, were returning this way in little groups. Minna hid from them when she heard the voices in the distance behind her and watched them pass from her hiding place in the bushes. Some were wounded, helped by their friends, but all were hurrying, afraid of being captured. Being captured would mean becoming a slave to the

Romans, not a happy prospect. No wonder they stumbled along, half-running, exhausted and demoralized. But if they were going this way, no doubt the men with Silva were taking the same road. Minna guessed she was not too far out in her calculations. Was there a base they were making for somewhere farther down the valley?

It grew dark and the familiar stars threw a silver web over the sky. A cold dew fell and Minna clutched the cloak around her, feeling desperately tired suddenly, and utterly dispirited. Only the company of dear Fortis, ever optimistic, encouraged her, keeping close to her side.

"I am really stupid, Fortis. I shall never find him!"

She tried to keep the sob out of her voice. She had done enough crying for the day. There were no more soldiers on the road now and the only sound was the cry of an owl from far in the forest. But the broken army was ahead of her somewhere and that was her only hope: that the men with Silva would be rested up with their fellows. So she plodded on.

Then Fortis stopped suddenly and growled low in his throat. Minna stopped too, with a lurch of fear.

"What is it?" she whispered.

She stooped to hold Fortis and could feel all the hair on his back raised in aggression. She crouched, listening.

Yes, there were voices ahead of her, not on the road but muffled by the forest somewhere on her right hand. She put the bridle reins around Fortis's throat to make a lead and whispered to him to keep silent. He knew commands and lay down, expectant. Minna felt her blood pulsing in her throat. If she were to be seen, she would be in great danger.

But she could not go back now. If there was a chance of finding Silva, surely he would be here among this group of fighters on the run… Holding Fortis tightly by the reins she crept as quietly as she could towards the sound of voices. She came to a beaten track off the road and followed it down, and soon saw the flickering of a fire in a clearing ahead of her. She pulled Fortis into the bushes and lay there, trying to see what was going on. It was very dark and hard to make out, but there seemed to be several men crouched over the flames, chattering in low voices. Beyond, on the edge of the clearing, there was a faint, lighter shape. Minna's heart lurched. Yes, it must be; she squinted up her eyes, staring. A flame suddenly sprang strongly out of the fire, just for a moment, and in that moment she saw that she had found Silva. He was tied to a tree on the far side of the clearing.

Her relief made her feel faint, almost collapsing with exhaustion and the whirling of her brain. She buried her head in her arms, trying not to sob with gratitude. How the gods had smiled on her! It was all she could do to stop herself from rushing across the glade to fling her arms around his neck.

But after the first rush of euphoria came the realization that to get him away from his captors was going to be extremely difficult. She must wait until they were all asleep, and then...she knew when he saw her, he would probably whinny. With Fortis crashing around as well, it was going to be almost impossible to steal him back without making a noise. She would have to wait until the men were deeply asleep. After such a day they should be exhausted. But as she lay there she saw that they were all in a state of shocked excitement, not ready to sleep in spite of physical exhaustion. She might have to wait some time before her chance came.

She wrapped her thick cloak around her and tried to rest. Her mind too was in a turmoil. She thought she would be lucky to succeed. If she didn't…she couldn't help dwelling on the possible outcome if the men captured her as well as Silva. Possibly having Fortis with her would be a bonus. She knew he would attack any man who attacked her. But he could also be a liability, barking with excitement when he saw Silva.

She was so tired she eventually slept heavily. She awoke with a start, how much later she had no idea. Was there a suggestion of dawn in the sky? The darkness was not so absolute and she could make out the shape of Silva on his tether, trying to reach some juicier grass just out of range. The men were huddled together by the ashes of the fire, heavily asleep judging by the snoring.

Now was her chance!

She could feel herself trembling already. She slipped out of the folds of the cloak – she would abandon that – and restrained Fortis, who was already up and ready to go, tail waving madly. She would just have to trust him to follow her and keep out of harm's way for she would need both hands for Silva. She pulled out her dagger from its sheath on her leg and picked up the bridle. Stood up.

Silva lifted his head.

Oh, Silva! Do not whinny! Do not make a sound!

But as she crept towards him past the huddled soldiers, she heard the soft welcoming whicker with which he always greeted her, a fluttering of the nostrils and the sound deep in his throat. One of the soldiers stirred as she stepped past him. Fortis gave a happy whimper. The soldier groaned.

Silva then let out a pleased whinny.

Minna flung herself at his tethering rope and felt that it was thick and strong.

Fortis barked, leaping about with excitement and the wakeful soldier let out some oaths, lifted himself on one elbow and stared blearily towards the action. Minna realized at once that the rope was too thick to cut quickly so threw off the head collar it was attached to, leaving Silva completely free. There was no time to bridle him. She heard the soldier shout the alarm and the others groan and struggle up to see what was going on, and she pulled Silva around to face them by the forelock and, holding the dagger in her teeth, vaulted onto his back. He was facing now in the direction she wanted, so she belted him with the bridle she still clutched, kicked him with all her strength, and held on for dear life as the startled horse reared into action. He jumped clean over the huddle of soldiers, but the one who had woken first was on his feet. In his hand he clutched an ax, and as Silva galloped away out of the glade he flung it after him with all his force.

Minna felt Silva lurch and almost fall. Dementedly she shouted at him, "Go, go, go, Silva!" and drummed him with her heels. He set off at a wild gallop down the path towards the road with Minna leaning over his withers to steer him by her hands on his neck. But she could feel by his action that he was hurt.

He knew the way home. Minna kept him going until she was far enough away from the men to be safe and then she talked him into a halt. She could tell with a sinking heart that he was only too ready to pull up. She slipped off his back in an agony of fear and stood back to see how he was injured.

The ax had caught him across the flank and made a huge, deep wound from which the blood was pouring. She could see there was no way to staunch it and that he was likely to die from loss of blood quite soon. Her only thought was to get him home into the hands of the Roman surgeons and the horsemaster as soon as possible. It was his only chance.

She fumbled the bridle into place and vaulted again onto his back. She knew he wanted to stay and be comforted, but she cruelly gave him a cut with the twirled reins and drummed her heels into his sides again. She could feel his surprise, shock, at her rough treatment but he broke into a canter immediately. She drummed with her heels harder and he started to gallop. Fortis flew alongside, his long legs keeping pace. Minna could see great gouts of blood spattering the dog's coat. She was full of despair, desperation. Her only hope was to get Silva home, yet the galloping must be making the blood run faster! What else could she do?

Dawn was breaking now and she could see the way quite clearly. The road seemed to go on forever. Had she really come this far last night? No wonder she had slept so soundly nearly all the night through. She kept thinking she had killed Silva. If she hadn't rescued him he would have lived a happy enough life with the peasants, for they would have known his value. They wouldn't have starved and beaten him. But by demanding him back into her care, she had caused him this terrible injury. Her mind was scrambled, her heart aching.

.uually she could feel that Silva no longer had the strength to gallop. But she could see in the distance the fort on its hillock and heard on the breeze the thread of the trumpet for arousal. A new day was starting, but Silva was dying beneath her, she could feel it.

The gallop slowed to a canter and then to a shuffling trot. But Minna still urged him on. As she rode she prayed to every god she could think of and willed her determination through her body into the failing horse.

XIV

Benoc stayed awake all night, as ordered. He knew that in the small hours, when life's ebb was at its lowest, Draco might slip away to join the shades in the hereafter, perhaps – who knew? – to find greater happiness than ever he had found on earth. So to deny him this release, Benoc sat by him, talking, shaking him gently by the shoulder, dribbling water into his mouth, willing him into consciousness. It was hard to know what was sleep and what was coma, but a few sighs and groans encouraged him. Benoc was used to sitting up all night when commanded, and knew it was wise to take a few

...de in the cold air to stop feeling drowsy. ...before dawn, standing outside the tent to watch the first pale glint of day in the sky, he was surprised to find Stuf coming up the rise from the vicus.

"Hey, Benoc. Is Draco still alive? I've given up trying to sleep. I thought I could slip in and see you while the commander still sleeps."

"He lives, yes."

"Thank the gods! And Theo – is he bad?"

"No, not in danger, unless he refuses to rest."

"He's lucky to be alive. Did you see it? Amazing! What a day! I've decided I shall come no farther with the army. I cannot stomach this killing. Moving through the countryside, making camp, coming to new places – yes, I've enjoyed the march, but when the whole object of it is the killing, that is what I cannot accept. I never want to see another day like yesterday."

Benoc shrugged. "You will go back to Camulodunum? Would that I could!"

"No. I want to stay here. I like this place."

Benoc was surprised. Then he laughed. "You know the commander is sending Minna back to Camulodunum? He'll probably decide to send you back with her, if he knows you are leaving us."

"He can't give me orders! Besides, it would need a whole bodyguard to escort Minna back to Camulodunum. She'll refuse to leave him. I can't find her, by the way. She seems to have disappeared, and Silva too, so I suppose she's taken him off for a ride to calm herself down. I was down there last night, but the old girls were asleep and there was no Minna, so I went over to the vicus to see if they were settling back again. They were celebrating the victory, so I joined in. They'd probably have celebrated if Kimbelinus had won too. It's all the same to them."

He stood for a moment, contemplating.

. "And so who is going to break it to Minna that she goes no farther with the army? When is he going to tell her?"

"When he can summon up the courage."

Stuf laughed. "Yes, defeating Kimbelinus's army will be as nothing compared to telling Minna she has to leave him."

"It will grieve him too. Equally, I think. He has put it off for so long."

Benoc's weary face revealed the burden he carried, of so closely, intimately, sharing his commander's life. Stuf had always thought that slaves, standing mutely behind their masters to take their next order, knew more of their domestic affairs and even of the affairs of state than most of the great men's closest friends.

Benoc said to him, "I think you should tell Minna. It will be easier for you to do it than for the commander. Go and see him now before he gets up. It will be a weight off his mind if you take it on yourself. He has more than enough to think about just now. The tribune from Melandra has been sent for and it will be a heavy day of politics when his retinue arrives. Go to him now."

Stuf, with some misgivings, went into the tent as Benoc lifted the flap aside for him. It wasn't large, filled mostly by a table with benches around it where meals were taken and conferences with the centurions held, and with chests that held all the army paraphernalia. But Draco lay prone on this table now and Theo was lying on a makeshift bed just inside the door. He opened his eyes as the light fell on him and blinked at Stuf.

Stuf, without preamble, said to him, "Benoc has just given me orders, sir, that I am to break the news to Minna that she will come no farther with the army. I am coming no farther either. This fighting is not for me. Shall I tell her?"

Theo groaned. He turned on his side and tried to rise but fell back with a curse at the pain.

"Benoc knows me well. It is true I haven't the courage to tell her. By Jupiter, I would rather face a dozen of Kimbelinus than face a crying woman! Yes, do this for me, Stuf! Minna – oh, my Minna!"

To Stuf's amazement he choked on what sounded like a sob and lay with his head buried in his arms. The first shaft of sunlight creeping in touched his prostrate body as if in a sympathetic caress. Stuf straightened up, bewildered. To his relief Benoc reappeared, carrying a leather bucket of hot water which he had fetched from the camp kitchen. He looked at Theo and showed no surprise at finding him apparently weeping. He shook him unceremoniously by the shoulder.

"The sun is up, sir."

Theo groaned. "Leave me, Benoc," he muttered, almost inaudibly. "A minute. I would speak with Stuf."

"Yes, sir."

Benoc gave Stuf the sideways glimmer of a smile and went out again.

Theo turned his head without attempting to rise

and said softly to Stuf, "Tell Minna – oh, what to tell Minna? Tell her I love her too much. She is to go back. Or go with you. I cannot take her. I cannot! She was not born to live this life. What happened yesterday is going to happen again. And again. It is not for her. She is only a child. She will forget me. I have known this all the time but have been too cowardly to tell her. And now I am still too cowardly, and I give the job to you, Stuf, since you offered. To tell her. Please. I am sorry."

Stuf found it hard to believe that this was the same Theo who went into battle without flinching, eyes alight, sword flashing; who suffered injury and hardship and hunger and pain without more than a curse at poor Benoc; who defied the authorities and always got what he wanted...a coward? He thought he was a coward!

"I will look after her, sir, do not worry."

Stuf almost wanted to embrace Theo to comfort him, seeing his despair. But he knew that his words were comfort enough. Theo's face lit into a smile of relief.

"That is wonderful news, Stuf! She will be in far better hands than mine, if she goes with you. Thank you. I thank you with all my heart."

Stuf retreated, overwhelmed with unfamiliar emotion. Benoc was waiting outside. Having been up all night, Benoc now had to see Theo washed, shaved, dressed, his wound seen to, his uniform cleaned, his breakfast delivered, orders taken, Draco nursed and washed and generally made to live...great grief! Who would be a slave? With the sun now creeping into the valley and the soldiers all around him waking with the familiar oaths and swearing and clamor, Stuf stood taking in the scene and swallowing great lungfuls of the glorious air, knowing he was a free man, answerable to no one, the only person, he believed, in the whole valley without a care in the world. He wanted to shout with joy. True, he had to sort out Minna...

But at that moment, as if on cue, there was a shout from the guards at the gate, and he saw Fortis flying up the hill towards him. Behind him came Minna, covered in blood, leading Silva who was head down, staggering with every step.

Minna was screaming, "Benoc! Benoc! Help me!"

Stuf ran to meet her.

"Get help for me, Stuf! Get the horsemaster – the surgeons! Benoc – and Benoc – please – to stop his bleeding! He is going to die!"

As she spoke, Silva went down, slumping to the ground right outside the commander's doorway. He gave a great groan and a few spasmodic kicks. Minna thought it was his last gasp and let out a scream which brought both Benoc and Theo out of the doorway.

"By all the gods! Whatever's going on?"

But Theo, without waiting for an answer, took one look at Silva and snapped out orders. In a moment men came running up from the animal lines. Immediately the horsemaster dropped to his knees and started to try and pull the gaping slash together with his hands, shouting orders. Men went running to do his bidding, fetching hot water from the kitchen and instruments and what was left of the clean linen from the hospital building.

"Silva! Silva! Don't die! Please don't die!"

Minna kneeled by Silva's head, talking softly into his ear. His eyes were shut and he kept shuddering, his breath coming short and fast. Minna wept.

"Please, Silva! Don't die!"

He was such a brave horse – surely he could hold off the terrible moment of passing into the afterworld? Not yet! He was only young.

"Don't go, Silva! Don't go!"

Then Minna felt arms around her as Theo lifted her up.

"Come, Minna, he cannot hear you just now. Leave him to the men who know their job. If he is to be saved, they will do it. Leave him. Come with me."

He led her into his quarters and sat her down on his still-warm bed. He was undressed and tousled and looked gaunt and exhausted. His wound was weeping painfully and Draco lay there as near death as Silva, and Minna gradually came to her senses and saw that the world did not revolve entirely around her horse. Benoc stood inscrutable, awaiting orders as always.

"Get her something to eat and drink, Benoc."

Benoc went out and Theo held Minna against his warm body. For once the embrace was not barricaded by the hard leather and metal of a uniform. It was a comfort that restored her senses so that her shuddering distress quietened and the world started to rearrange itself. Not only a horse was dying that day.

"It was terrible," she whispered. "Yesterday was terrible."

"Yes."

"And Draco?"

"I don't know. Benoc has been tending him all night."

They got up and went to Draco's side. His face was white and bloodless, his lips tinged with blue, but his breathing was even and deep. As if he felt their presence, his eyes opened and focused on them. Minna thought she saw all manner of doubts and horrors shadowed in their depths, as if his mind were clear, but perhaps it was her imagination.

Theo put a hand on the boy's shoulder and said softly, "Get well, Draco, you have a splendid future ahead of you. I honor you for saving my life. Your desertion is forgiven and will never be spoken of. We love you and need you. You must recover."

There was an urgency in his last words, the voice of the commander.

Draco's eyes closed. But the faintest smile moved across his lips.

"Benoc will save him," Theo said.

To Minna he looked as bad as Silva.

Benoc brought in a bowl of hot gruel and a beaker of some concoction that burned Minna's mouth and set fire to her breast. She felt herself recovering, felt her optimism returning, sat herself down and started devouring the gruel. How hungry she was! She had never noticed until the food was set before her. Benoc turned his attention to Theo and made him lie down on the bed while he redressed the wound. Minna didn't look. She had had enough of blood. But Benoc seemed satisfied with its progress and, having bound it up again with fresh linen, he dressed Theo in his clean, unbloodied uniform and set out his shaving tools. Theo ran his thumb over the flake of flintstone Benoc used and said, "Sharpen it, Benoc. I don't want any more cuts today than those I already have."

Minna went to the doorway, stumbling now with weariness. The men had finished working on Silva and she could see that he was still breathing. The terrible wound had been forced into closure and was held with straining stitches beneath a covering of woundwort leaves and linen. Blood still trickled down over his hind legs, which were black with dried blood. His beautiful tail was full of blood, drying it into a dark fan over the grass. The sun was coming up over the hillside and the camp was stirring with all the familiar sounds and smells of daybreak, as if the dreadful day of battle had never happened. The carnage was hidden in the valley below the walls and Minna did not look that way. She squatted beside Silva's head and stroked his damp neck. His eyes were closed, his nostrils flaring with every weak breath. Fortis came to her side, his tail dragging, and licked her hands.

Minna could no longer think straight, exhausted by emotion.

Theo came out and the trumpet shrilled its familiar fanfare for the men to fall in. Theo went down to the drilling ground with his centurions and the day started as usual. Stuf appeared and stood silently, looking down at Silva.

After a little while he said, "He's chosen a fine place to get sick, right in the doorway of the commander's quarters. There will be no moving him for a while, by the look of it."

Benoc came out and said to Minna, "The commander said you can rest in his bed, to stay near Silva."

He lifted the coverings over the horse's wound and considered it, pursing his lips. Then he went back and came out with the bottle of stuff he had used on Theo, and poured the contents over the wound. He replaced the linen.

"That's the best," he said. "He will live."

"Go and sleep," Stuf said gently to Minna. "I will watch over your horse. And Benoc will nurse him."

Minna stumbled gratefully back into the building and sank into the covers that were pulled aside. The bed was no softer than the earth she was used to lying on, but it bore Theo's imprint and the smell of his weary body and Minna felt his spirit all around her.

She slept.

XV

Benoc brought his two charges, Draco and Silva, back from the brink of death. He kept going with scarcely any sleep, animated by a brew from the army hospital generally used for soldiers on guard duty. Stuf helped him, but Minna was forced to go back to her shelter. A girl was not wanted around the commander's quarters, not with the coming and going of Roman visitors from Melandra and Deva who came to celebrate the fort's return into their hands.

Draco was moved into a bed in the hospital quarters and Silva, when he at last staggered to his feet, went to join his friend Caractacus in the horse lines. Minna stayed there with him, tending him, bringing him tidbits, cleaning the last specks of blood out of his tail. His winter coat was just starting to grow and as his gaunt body began to fill out again he began to look like the horse he once was. Soon he would be moving on with the army towards the North. Minna worked hard to build up his strength so that he would not be too weak for the journey. Theo was so busy Minna scarcely saw him.

Stuf bided his time to tell Minna that she was not going any farther with the army. It was only one day, when he found her sitting in the grass beside the grazing Silva and she remarked that the horse was now fit enough to keep up on the march, that he hunkered down beside her and told her of Theo's decision.

"He will not take you any farther, Minna. He says there is no place for you with the army. He does not want you to see another battle. He wants you to be safe and happy. I told him I liked it here and was going to stay and he asked me to look after you. Or take you home if you wish. I said I would."

Minna stared at him in disbelief.

"He doesn't want me any more?"

"For your own sake, Minna. To stay safe. He wept because he is going on without you, because he loves you too much to take you into the fighting. He wants you to go home. And he loves you, Minna. He wept because he loves you so and you have to part."

He thought he might have exaggerated slightly, but the gist of it was true, tempered to the reception it was likely to get from Minna.

She just stared at him, aghast.

"Go home? How can we part? How can I go home?"

"With an escort, easily. He will provide one."

"I can't go home. It's not possible. I can't leave him."

"Stay here then. I'm going to stay here. You can too. It's a nice place to settle."

Minna lay back, staring at the sky. She did not speak for some time. Stuf waited patiently.

"He *said* he loves me? He said it?"

"Yes. He said it. To me. He cried, Minna. Because he loves you so."

"He has never said it to me. Not properly."

"No. Because he cannot offer you anything, Minna.

Only battles, and who wants more of that? Only Theo."

"And he told you he loved me?"

"Yes. Minna, he did. I'm going to make some breakfast. I've got some eggs. Would you like some if I cook them?"

"Yes."

He left her still lying, staring at the sky. Fortis bounded at his side. Silva shook himself and went to join Caractacus, who was already grazing.

It was a beautiful morning. Minna thought she must still be dreaming, the news that Stuf had spilled in such a matter-of-fact manner almost impossible to take in. Theo loved her. She had to go home. He loved her. They had to part. He loved her. He *cried*. He loved her! The words went round and round in her head. Far, far at the back of her mind, it did not surprise her that he said they must part, and a part of her thanked the gods that she did not have to face the horrors of the North, that she could stay behind in this beautiful valley. With Stuf? Hadn't he said he was going to stay? Even if she insisted on going with the army, she knew Theo would never again repeat that he loved her. He would hold her at arm's length as he had always done.

And probably, through anger at her disobedience, tire of her and start to hate her.

She could not argue with his decision. There truly hadn't been any alternative. She had never brought herself to face it before. But the thought of never seeing him again after he departed was terrible. She wished she had been the one to jump between him and Kimbelinus's sword and take the dire wound which had saved his life. And to die for him. That would show him how much she loved him!

But as she lay there looking up at the sky she realized that she really did not want to die. Not yet. There was comfort in the thought of staying put and making some sort of a home in this valley. And the way back to her old home in Othona would always be open, when she was too old to marry Esca but not too old to see her mother again. And who knew but that Theo might come back, perhaps injured too badly to serve any longer, raised to a government role, perhaps to leave the army altogether? And she would still be there. Or he might be killed and she would not have him anyway. Her thoughts wandered and the hysterics she knew Stuf had dreaded were not forthcoming. She just repeated to herself over and over Stuf's words:

He loves you, Minna. He cried. They were the sweetest words she had ever heard.

Stuf shouted to her and she got up and wandered over to where he had made a small fire from some old ashes.

He handed her two eggs, boiled hard. She started to peel them. What a strange day!

"If you stay here," she said to Stuf, "what will you do?"

"Clear a piece of land, build a house, grow my food, have a few animals, enjoy myself, find a beautiful girl, marry her, have ten children, live to be old and respected, loved and cared for by my family...what else? I can't think of anything nicer."

"Huh! And if I stay here, what would I do?"

"You could do my cooking and cleaning and dig my garden until I find this beautiful girl to marry. You could sleep in the outhouse with the animals and I would bring you a share of the meal in the evening."

His face was quite serious. Minna was not sure if he were joking or not. Once, she remembered, she had suggested to her mother that she would rather marry Stuf than anyone else. If one married for good sense, instead of for love, marrying Stuf was a good idea.

Certainly she loved Stuf in a brotherly way; he had always been as a brother to her, right from childhood. She depended on him utterly. But right from childhood she had loved Theo too. And that was quite different.

She knew, in her heart, and had always known, that loving Theo was only a dream, and there was no future in it. But the fact now that he too acknowledged the same love and had spoken of it to Stuf meant that the parting, terrible though it would be, would leave her in peace.

After a little while she said, "I'm not a very good cook."

Stuf, amazed that she had taken his news so calmly, laughed and said, "Never mind. I am."

And then Minna remembered Silva, and knew that the parting from Silva was going to be just as dreadful as the parting from Theo. And she became the weeping woman that Theo had been so frightened of, and she went back to Silva and buried her face in his lovely mane and wept her heart out.

A week later the army was ready to march again. Theo had been forced to rest when he could to allow his wound to heal more fully and Benoc himself had given him cautious permission to travel again.

"To ride, sir. The men will understand. Until it's properly knit together."

"Yes, doctor. I will ride." He laughed. "I would that I could free you, Benoc, to stay behind. That's what you most want, what you deserve. But I need you too much."

"I would rather serve you, sir."

"You say that, like a good slave, but you deserve better. You got Draco to live, against his will; that was brilliant. He will ride in a wagon until he can walk and one day when he's a centurion he will be glad. You will guard him for now as you guard me, Benoc, and I will see that you are rewarded."

"Yes, sir."

"We go then. Get me dressed. Then the farewells. I wish we were away."

Benoc knew he dreaded saying goodbye to Minna. Since he had broken down after the battle, it was as if he had said his farewell to Minna, via Stuf. He had not seen her alone since. Benoc thought he could not trust himself. But now there was no escape. The camp was all dismantled, save for his tent, and the men stood by waiting, with the last baggage wagon. All the others were already loaded down in the road, the oxen hitched and the train of mules and donkeys waiting. His centurions had lined up their men in marching order and one of the soldier grooms was waiting with Caractacus tacked up.

Benoc fastened Theo into his breastplate and ornate belt, handed him his helmet and his sword, and Theo went out. It was a fine sunny day early in the morning, the flush of summer over and the nip of autumn in the air. The people in the vicus had lined up beyond the wall, not sure if they were glad or sorry to see the army go, and Minna and Stuf stood in the gateway with some of the elderly retainers and the more badly wounded who were going to stay behind. Theo walked down the slope towards them.

Minna steeled herself to be as brave as Draco, as Theo himself. How magnificent he looked, the plume on his helmet lifting in the faintest breeze, the deep scar over his eye still unable to spoil the arrogant beauty of his features! Minna, severely lectured by Stuf, watched him coolly as he bade farewell to his men and commended them for their faithful service. She held her breath. He came to Stuf, shook him warmly by the hand, then stood before her.

"Minna," he said. "Goodbye."

"Goodbye, Theo." Her voice did not shake.

He reached out and took her hands and lifted them up to his lips and kissed them.

"I shall never forget you."

"No," she whispered.

"I'm leaving you a present."

"A present?"

She looked up. He was signaling to someone behind the gateway. Minna heard a whinny and a soldier came out from behind the wall leading Silva. He came up the slope, saluted, and put the reins in Minna's hands.

Theo said, "I've retired him from the army. He's yours."

Minna was speechless. The prospect of losing Silva had been as hideous in her mind as the prospect of losing Theo, but this was something she had never envisaged.

"Theo!"

She made an instinctive leap – she could not help herself – to fling her arms around him, heard Stuf squawk at her, felt the hard metal of Theo's armor pressing painfully against her body, his lips on hers, hard and fierce, then he had spun around, vaulted onto Caractacus and was suddenly at the head of his cohort, the trumpet signal breaking out and the hillside suddenly alive as the centurions barked out orders to march and the army moved off.

Silva let out a great whinny as he saw his friend Caractacus depart without him, but Minna held him hard and cried to him, "You must lose him too, Silva, like me! They've got to go!"

She was both laughing and crying together. The army marched past her, looking magnificent, some of the men giving her a sympathetic smile, and at their head rode Theo on Caractacus, not looking back.

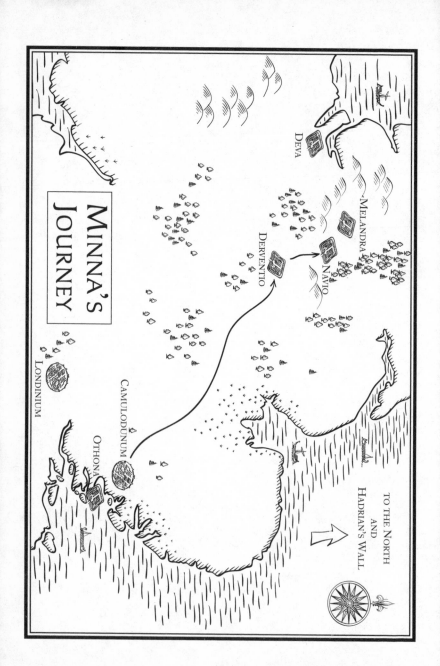

GLOSSARY

amphora – a pottery jar, bulbous in shape with a narrow neck, pointed base and two handles, used to store and transport items

Balkerne Gate – the large western gate in Camulodunum's perimeter wall, the remains of which can still be seen today

Brigantes – a Celtic warrior tribe who controlled a large part of northern England and the Midlands before the Romans arrived in Britain

Caledonia – Scotland. The Romans named the area after the local Celtic tribe, the Caledones

Camulodunum – Colchester, Essex

Caractacus – British chieftain who resisted the Roman invasion of AD43. Son of Cunobelin

centurion – a professional solider, officer of the Roman army, who commanded eighty soldiers and twenty support personnel

cohort – a unit of the Roman army consisting of 480 soldiers (divided into six centuries of eighty men, each commanded by a centurion)

Derventio – a Roman fort which was located at a place now known as Little Chester, Derby

Deva – Chester, Cheshire

gladius – the Roman name for a sword

Hadrian – Roman emperor from AD117–138, who ordered the construction of a great wall to safeguard northern England against invasion from Caledonia (Scotland)

Jupiter – the chief god in Roman mythology, in charge of laws and social order

legion – a division of the Roman army consisting of about five thousand soldiers

Londinium – London

Melandra – a small Roman fort, also known as Ardotalia, the remains of which can still be seen near Glossop, in the Peak District

Mithras – the god of Mithraism, an Eastern Mediterranean religion practiced in the Roman Empire, particularly popular with soldiers

Navio – a Roman fort, a few remains of which still survive at Brough-on-Noe, Derbyshire

Othona – a Roman fort which was located in an isolated area of what is now Essex

pilum (plural pila) – a Roman javelin with a long, pointed iron head and a wooden shaft. The small point could penetrate a shield and even pierce armor

standard – a military emblem carried on a pole

Stane Street – a Roman road leading west from Camulodunum (Colchester) into what is now Hertfordshire

stockade – a tall fence made of logs placed side by side with the tops sharpened. Used as a form of defense in Roman military camps and settlements, or for confining animals

tribune – a high-ranking official in either the army or government

vicus (plural vici) – a civilian settlement which grew up close to a Roman military garrison

ALSO BY K.M. PEYTON

MINNA'S QUEST

Minna is just a blacksmith's daughter, yet she succeeds in raising a sickly abandoned foal, turning him into the pride of the Roman cavalry. Her stubborn determination and fiery nature burn brightly in the quiet fort of Othona and soon attract the secret admiration of the proud commander Theo.

But even Theo cannot imagine the part Minna and her beloved horse will play when Othona is threatened by bloodythirsty pirates. Desperate to save her people, Minna risks all as she sets out on a perilous journey over land and wave to find help.

"A gripping adventure, tautly written." *The Guardian*

NO TURNING BACK

Roman servant girl Minna has run away to the big city on her beloved horse, Silva. Hopelessly in love with the courageous commander Theo, her only thought is to gain his admiration – whatever it takes.

Spying a magnificent horse stolen from the Roman army, she sees her chance: steal back the stallion and win Theo's heart. But the horse is guarded by a wild band of thieves led by a ruthless warrior, and when Minna puts her plan into action, she sparks a deadly chain of events from which there can be no turning back.

Usborne Quicklinks

For links to websites where you can find out more about Roman life in Britain, dress a Roman soldier in his armor, and see pictures of what Colchester (Camulodunum) would have looked like in Roman times, go to the Usborne Quicklinks Website at www.usborne-quicklinks.com and enter the keywords "far from home".

Internet safety

When using the Internet, make sure you follow these safety guidelines:

- Ask an adult's permission before using the Internet.
- Never give out personal information, such as your name, address or telephone number.
- If a website asks you to type in your name or e-mail address, check with an adult first.
- If you receive an e-mail from someone you don't know, don't reply to it.